"You're running, Memory. You're running from me *and* from yourself," Drew told her.

She looked up at him, eyes full of anger and pain. "I am *not* running, Drew Sloan. I'm . . ." She stopped. "All right, I *am* running. I won't deny it because it's true. Yes, you turn me on, is that what you want to hear? Does it give your ego a rush? It's just physical, Drew—is a roll in the hay what you wanted?"

"Knock it off, Memory. There's nothing cheap or sordid about what's happening between us. This is real and honest between us. It's good, Memory."

"It's nothing," she insisted.

"You're wrong." He moved his hand from her arm to the nape of her neck and lowered his head. "I want you, Memory," Drew murmured, his lips against hers. "I've never wanted anyone as much as I do you. . . ."

WHAT ARE *LOVESWEPT* ROMANCES?

They are stories of true romance and touching emotion. We believe those two very important ingredients are constants in our highly sensual and very believable stories in the *LOVESWEPT* line. Our goal is to give you, the reader, stories of consistently high quality that may sometimes make you laugh, sometimes make you cry, but are always fresh and creative and contain many delightful surprises within their pages.

Most romance fans read an enormous number of books. Those they truly love, they keep. Others may be traded with friends and soon forgotten. We hope that each *LOVESWEPT* romance will be a treasure—a "keeper." We will always try to publish

LOVE STORIES YOU'LL NEVER FORGET
BY AUTHORS YOU'LL ALWAYS REMEMBER

The Editors

Loveswept ® 594

Joan Elliott Pickart
Angels Singing

BANTAM BOOKS
NEW YORK · TORONTO · LONDON · SYDNEY · AUCKLAND

ANGELS SINGING

A Bantam Book / February 1993

If you would be interested in receiving protective vinyl
covers for your Loveswept books, please write to this address
for information:

Loveswept
Bantam Books
P.O. Box 985
Hicksville, NY 11802

ISBN 0-553-44361-5

Published simultaneously in the United States and Canada

Bantam Books are published by Bantam Books, a division of
Bantam Doubleday Dell Publishing Group, Inc. Its trademark,
consisting of the words "Bantam Books" and the portrayal of
a rooster, is Registered in U.S. Patent and Trademark Office
and in other countries. Marca Registrada. Bantam Books, 666
Fifth Avenue, New York, New York 10103.

PRINTED IN THE UNITED STATES OF AMERICA

OPM   0 9 8 7 6 5 4 3 2 1

For Greg

One

He had never heard that sound before, yet there was no doubt whatsoever in Drew Sloan's mind that the crisp, metallic snap had been the cocking of the hammer of a gun. He froze where he was hunkered down, his hands still on the strap of the backpack he'd slipped off and placed on the ground.

With the beat of his thundering heart roaring in his ears, he waited. Only noises of nature reached him—the chill wind whistling through trees, birds calling to one another, the muted chattering of a squirrel.

Seconds ticked by with maddening slowness, and sweat trickled down his back.

If his life was passing before his eyes, he thought, he was becoming too angry to notice the mental movie. Enough was enough.

"So?" he said, not shifting his position an inch. "What's the plan? Are you going to blow my head off now, or do I get to make one phone call first?"

"Raise your hands and get to your feet. Do it slow and easy."

A woman? he thought incredulously. That had definitely been a female voice. He was being held at gunpoint by a woman. It was a serious blow to his ego that someone had snuck up on him in the first place. He prided himself on his abilities to act in concert with nature, and all of his senses had been honed to razor sharpness.

Well, not this time, he thought. Whoever this gun-totin' mama was, she'd caught him totally unawares. Hell.

"Mister," the woman said, "move it. *Now!*"

Drew sighed and raised his hands to shoulder level, slowly straightening until he was standing up. His jaw was set in a tight, angry clench.

"Turn toward me," the woman said. "Any quick moves and, believe me, you'll regret it."

He muttered an earthy expletive as he followed the instructions. When he was fully turned, he said, "This is ridiculous. I really resent—"

He stopped speaking as he forgot what he really resented. His eyes widened as he stared at the woman standing about ten feet in front of him.

Yes, she was pointing a gun at him, a single-barrel shotgun to be more precise. And yes, the hammer was cocked, just as he'd thought.

Next to her was a gray and black German

shepherd, a huge German shepherd, that looked as though he gobbled up six-foot, two-hundred-pound men such as Drew as a tasty appetizer before lunch.

All those details registered in Drew's brain within seconds, before his full attention was centered on the woman herself.

She was one of the most stunning feminine creations he had ever had the pleasure of feasting his eyes on.

She was tall, around five foot ten, he guessed, wore faded jeans on slender legs that went from here to next week, and a blue plaid flannel shirt that couldn't quite hide her full breasts.

Her hair was a wild but attractive mane that tumbled in waves to her shoulders, and was as black and glossy as polished ebony.

And her face . . . Lord, she was beautiful. He somehow knew she wore no makeup, that the glow of her skin was natural. Her eyes were large and dark and framed in long lashes that some women would kill for. Her nose was cute, like a little girl's, and that kept her beauty from being too perfect, too daunting. But her lips . . . Her lips were perfection, shaped to be kissed, and kissed, and—

"What are you doing here?" she asked, jolting him from his reverie.

He could look at this woman all day, Drew thought, frowning, and not consider it a hardship. But talk to her? Forget it. She was pushy, brash, rude, and had a personality about as pleasant as a turnip.

"I'm hiking, your highness," he said, making no attempt to curb his sarcasm. "The last time I checked, there was no law against it, so point that shotgun of yours at something else."

"There *is* a law against trespassing," she said. "Keep those hands up."

"My fingers are going numb. All the blood is draining from my hands and arms. This is nuts. What do you think, that I've got a machine gun in the pocket of my windbreaker? You may be into acting out a role in a grade B movie, but I can live without it. And I'm *not* trespassing."

"You most certainly are," she shot back. "This is *my* land, *my* mountain, you tromped over."

"Mountain? Try 'hill,' lady. It's fairly good size, but not close to being a mountain."

"Listen, Mr. Whoever-you-are, you're standing on Memory Mountain and every square inch of it is mine."

"Sloan. It's Drew Sloan, and I'm putting my hands down right now, Miss Memory Mountain."

"Fine, you may lower your hands, but don't try anything tricky."

"Oh, brother," he muttered, rolling his eyes as he dropped his hands to his sides.

"And it's Memory Lawson."

"What is?"

"My name."

"You mean this hill—excuse me, this mountain was named after you?"

"Yes, and you are most definitely trespassing."

"There aren't any signs posted saying that this is private property."

"Well, it is. Now you know it, so pick up your gear and be on your way."

"What's your dog's name?" he asked, glancing at the large animal. "I mean, you have an unusual name. I just wondered if your dog did too."

"His name is Dog. Good-bye, Mr. Sloan."

Memory tightened her hold on the shotgun, hoping that Drew Sloan would do as he was told and just leave. Even with a deep frown on his face, he was much too handsome for her peace of mind. He wasn't movie-star handsome, but his rugged features—the square jaw, prominent cheekbones, broad forehead—were undeniably attractive. As was his thick brown hair, tousled by the rising wind, and his dark eyes, the color of chocolate chips.

But, she told herself, he was a typical weekend hiker, all decked out in his two-hundred-dollar boots, brand new jeans, navy blue sweatshirt, and matching windbreaker emblazoned with the logo of an expensive sports clothes designer.

She knew his type. He walked around for a while, took photographs every fifty feet, stopped for rest breaks every half mile, then come Monday morning at the office, he'd tell everyone who would listen about his perilous mountain climbing and communing with nature.

A phony, she thought, with a sniff of disgust. Drop-dead gorgeous, but as phony as a three-dollar bill.

She started when she heard him say her name, and realized he'd been trying to get her attention while she'd been staring at him.

"May I call you Memory?" he went on. "It really is a pretty name. Anyway . . . Memory, would you mind aiming that shotgun at something other than my person? I've been inhabiting this body for thirty-two years, and I've grown rather fond of it. Besides, my mother would be disconsolate if you shot me dead. You wouldn't want to upset my sweet little mom, would you?"

Mother? Memory mentally repeated. Did that mean there wasn't a Mrs. Drew Sloan? Oh, for Pete's sake, who cared?

"All right," she said. She uncocked the shotgun, then pointed the barrel toward the ground. "Now go." She flapped her free hand at him. "Get off my mountain. Go home to your mother."

He crossed his arms over his chest. "I don't live with my mother. What do you take me for, a mama's boy? That's really insulting, Memory."

"I'm sorry, but you did say . . ." She blinked. "Why am I apologizing to you? *You're* the one who's trespassing on *my* land. Good-bye, Mr. Sloan."

He didn't want to leave, Drew suddenly realized.

Memory Lawson was fascinating, beautiful, and feisty, and obviously comfortable in nature's arena. That final attribute was a big one, since he'd decided years ago that the woman he married had to enjoy the out-of-doors as much as he. Of course, he didn't expect her to be as adept at camping, hiking, white-water rafting, and such as he was, but the enthusiasm had to be there.

So far, the selection of women with that mind-set had been slim to the point of being nonexistent. But there stood Memory Lawson, protecting her mountain with a shotgun and a dog named Dog. Beautiful Memory Lawson. Who had, he reminded himself in the next second, a personality that grated on his nerves like nails scratching on a chalkboard.

Then again, maybe she wasn't always so crabby. Surely she didn't go through life in a constant state of grouchiness. Well, there was only one way to find out. He simply had to concoct a plan by which he could hang around for a while. Think, Sloan.

"Well," he said, smiling to beat the band, "it certainly was an experience meeting you, Memory. If it ever comes up in conversation, I'll be able to say I met a woman in northern Arizona who had a hill . . . pardon me . . . a mountain named after her." *Brain, where are you?* "Yes, sir, it's not every day of the week that a man—"

"Good-bye, Mr. Sloan."

His smile faded, and he began to walk backward.

"Yeah, right. I'm gone. See ya, Dog. Have a nice day, Memory, and—"

"Watch out!" she yelled.

"What—"

In the next few seconds, Drew realized two things. One was that he'd forgotten that his backpack was lying on the ground. The second was that the ground making up Memory Mountain was extremely hard. He'd instinctively shot out his right hand as he fell, and fiery pain radiated from the tips of his fingers all the way up to his shoulder.

"Oh-h-h," he moaned, clutching his arm. "Dammit, I don't believe this."

Memory flipped the safety catch into place on the shotgun, then hurried to Drew's side. She dropped to her knees with Dog right beside her and set the shotgun on the ground.

"Oh-h-h," he moaned again.

"Would you hush for a minute?" she said crossly. "All that noise isn't going to solve anything."

Drew glowered at her. "Your beside manner is not what I'd call state-of-the-art. I'm injured, wounded, in terrible pain. I killed my arm, dammit."

"You'd better not be faking this," she said, "or your nose is going to feel the way you're pretending that your arm does."

"I'm not faking," he yelled, then moaned again.

He wished he *was* faking, wished that a mock injury had been his extraordinarily intelligent plan to stay there for a while, get to know Memory better. But the pain was all too real. He'd really clobbered himself, and made a fool of himself in the process. Dandy.

"Let go of your arm," she said, "so I can see how badly you're hurt."

"No."

"Okay, fine. Just stay put and moan your little heart out. The only problem is that you're still trespassing on my mountain."

"You're cold," he said sullenly. "You don't have a heart, it's an ice cube. Where's your compassion?"

"Darned if I know. Are you going to let me check your arm or not?"

"I suppose," he said, slowly removing his hand. "But be gentle." He remained supine on the ground, his throbbing arm across his chest.

"Oh, don't be such a baby. Men strut their machismo at every opportunity, but the minute they get hurt, they act like little boys."

"Is that so?" Drew said. He slid a glance at her. "What makes you such an all-time expert on male behavior? Does your husband turn into a whining wimp when he bangs himself up?"

"I'm not married. I never have been."

Bingo, Drew thought. That was great news.

"I don't intend to ever marry."

That was *not* great news.

"My analysis of men," she went on, "comes from interacting with and observing them during my twenty-six years on this earth. Generally speaking, men are ridiculous. They are also the weaker sex."

"Nice attitude," Drew said dryly, "but could you skip the feminist sermonette? I'm in pain here, remember?"

. They exchanged glares, then Memory gently probed Drew's hand with her fingertips. When she reached his wrist, he yelped. Dog growled.

"Hush, Dog," Memory said, "and you hush, too, Sloan. You have a broken wrist. I'm guessing it's a clean break, nothing to make a fuss over."

"Nothing?" he hollered. "You call a broken wrist nothing?" He clutched his arm again and struggled to sit up. "Nothing, she says. I'm maimed, for crying out loud. Where's the nearest hospital?"

"About thirty-five miles from here." She stood and picked up the shotgun. "They'll put a pretty cast on your war wound and that'll be that. They might even give you a lollipop if you don't yell the roof down."

Drew slowly and carefully got to his feet, moaning the whole time. As soon as he was upright, a wave of dizziness swept over him. He swayed, closing his eyes.

"Hey, easy there," Memory said, placing one hand on his shoulder. "You're not going to pass out on me, are you?" She leaned closer. "Drew?"

He opened his eyes and met her gaze, their faces

only inches apart. The wind gusted around them as the temperature began to drop, but neither noticed. Dog flopped onto the ground, resting his chin on his paws, but neither noticed. Dark clouds rolled toward them, but neither noticed.

They simply stood there, seemingly suspended in time, not moving, hardly breathing, as they stared at each other.

Memory suddenly became aware of the taut muscles of Drew's shoulder, where her hand still rested. Heat radiated from his body to her palm and traveled up her arm, suffusing her chest and filling her breasts with a heavy ache.

She told herself to tear her gaze from Drew's, to remove her hand, to step away. But she was held immobile, and panic engulfed her.

"Memory," he said quietly, her name nearly carried beyond hearing by the wind.

His voice released her. She jerked her hand from his shoulder and took two steps back.

"You're a beautiful woman, do you know that?" he went on, his voice still hushed.

"So I've been told," she said coolly. "Men place a great deal of importance on that. What does she look like? That's always the first consideration."

Drew frowned. "You certainly have a chip on your shoulder about men. You *are* a beautiful woman, Memory. I'm not going to apologize for appreciating and commenting on that fact."

"Forget it." She sighed. "I suppose your vehicle,

wherever it is, doesn't have an automatic transmission."

"It's about five miles from here and, no, it has four-wheel drive and a standard transmission." An expression of pure innocence settled over his face as he smiled. "My goodness, I can't possibly drive myself to the hospital, can I?"

As she scowled at him, Drew's smile widened. She really was beautiful, he thought. He'd nearly kissed her a minute ago, nearly hauled her to him and pressed his mouth to her delectable lips. And that maneuver would no doubt have gotten his other arm broken.

"I'd call a taxi," he added when she didn't speak, "but I don't see a telephone booth up here on your mountain, ma'am."

"You're cute, Sloan, very cute. I'm amazed you actually hiked five miles. Well, I guess I'll have to drive you to the hospital in Tumbleweed."

"Don't knock yourself out," he said, then his smile faded as he repeated, "Tumbleweed? The dinky little town I passed through? The whole thing was only a block long, and I sure didn't see a hospital."

"It's not exactly a hospital, it's more of a clinic. A major injury or illness has to be tended in Williams. The clinic can certainly handle a simple little matter like your broken wrist, though." She turned and started away, Dog falling into place beside her.

"Hey, wait a minute," Drew said.

She stopped and looked at him over one shoulder. "Now what?"

"I can't cradle my arm and tote my backpack too. If I hold my wrist tightly to my chest it doesn't hurt so much. The weight of the backpack pulling on my shoulders wouldn't feel terrific."

"In other words, you want me to carry your backpack."

"Well . . ." He paused, then shook his head. "No, that's not a good idea. It's much too heavy for you. I'll wear it if you'll help me get it on."

She stalked past him, placed the shotgun on the ground, and moments later had the pack settled securely and properly on her back. She retrieved the shotgun and started off again.

"Let's go," she said, not looking at Drew as she passed him. "Close your mouth, Sloan, or something will fly into it."

Drew snapped his mouth closed, for it had indeed dropped open as he'd witnessed the ease with which Memory had handled his backpack.

He started after her, clutching his injured wrist, and glowering at Memory as her long legs took her quickly over the rocky terrain.

So what if Memory was strong, he thought. So what if she'd lifted the backpack as though it were filled with feathers. And the way she was walking? Hell, she was streaking along like she was trying to win a race.

Well, a lot she knew. A person had to pace himself on rough ground like this. She was obviously strutting her feminist stuff, her I'm-as-good-as-you-any-day-of-the-week-buster bit. She'd soon run out of steam and wilt before his very eyes.

He was an expert on the proper methods to hike, climb, camp, a whole range of skills necessary for surviving in the wilds. She'd get her comeuppance in no time at all.

In the meanwhile he'd enjoy the view in front of him—Memory's long, shapely legs encased in those tight jeans and the enticing glimpse of a curving bottom that peeked from beneath the tail of her flannel shirt.

Oh, yes, he mused, a very nice view. And the heat coiling low in his body was diverting his attention from the grinding pain that encompassed his entire arm all the way to his shoulder.

When a particularly cold gust of wind swept over them, Drew glanced up at the sky. Dark clouds were rapidly gathering over them, and he shook his head in resignation. Of course it was going to rain. It would be a fitting touch to his lousy day.

Again his gaze was caught by the intriguing woman walking ahead of him. Well, the day wasn't a total loss.

On they trekked, Drew mentally measuring the distance and proud of his ability to do so. He was not, of course, proud of having fallen over his own backpack like a jerk, but what was done was done. He'd redeem himself by not hassling Memory when she had to rest.

Any second now, she'd begin to slow her step, then would finally stop. He'd be a nice guy about it, despite the pain in his arm. He'd be patient and understanding.

Memory strode on by rote. She knew the terrain so well, it wasn't necessary for her to watch for unexpected obstacles in her path.

Usually, she enjoyed the chance to allow her thoughts to float free as she went for long walks with Dog. More often than not, she dwelled on nothing, just blanked her mind and soaked up the beauty of nature.

But at that moment, she wished her complete concentration was needed on the ground and her feet.

She did not want to think at all, because to do so was to face the fact that she was behaving like a shrew toward Drew Sloan. She'd been just plain nasty more than once, and totally unsympathetic about his broken wrist.

She had no choice, though, she reasoned. Drew was a compelling, handsome man, whose masculine magnetism was nearly a palpable entity. When he'd pinned her in place with those mesmerizing brown eyes of his, she'd been unable to move and barely able to breathe.

Drew Sloan was dangerous, and her only option was to build a solid barrier between them, a barrier constructed by her sharp words and haughty attitude. The wall was fulfilling its assignment,

too, for Drew glowered and glared at her more
often than he smiled.

And that smile . . . Memory stifled a sigh. Drew
Sloan had a devastating smile. It lit up his face
like sunshine after a storm, and his dark eyes
became sparkling, inviting pools.

He was the epitome of man, she thought, and
she wanted him off her mountain and out of her
life as quickly as he'd appeared. He represented
exactly what she would never fall prey to again.

Two

Ten minutes later Drew begrudgingly, but silently, admitted that Memory Mountain was entitled to its name. It was definitely *not* just a good-size hill. His ascent on the other side had been gradual, requiring little physical effort, but Memory was now leading him back down in the opposite direction.

She was exercising the proper method of descending a steep incline, shifting sideways, then firmly planting one foot before moving the other. So, okay, she knew something about hiking, but she was still going too fast. Memory Lawson would pay the piper and holler for a rest very soon now.

Ten more minutes passed.

Drew hugged his arm tighter to his chest. The firm placing of his feet jolted the arm, intensifying the pain. He gave Memory's back a dark glare, then mentally threw up his hands in defeat.

"Okay, okay," he said. "Hold it, Flash, I need a break. I'm an injured man, remember?"

She stopped and looked up at him. Dog did the same.

"Oh," she said. "Tired, are we?"

"No, we are not tired. We are in pain, and we would appreciate the opportunity to take a breather."

He moved to a large, semiflat rock and sat down, sighing deeply.

Memory stared at him for a long moment, then walked slowly upward and settled next to him. Dog flopped down on the ground by her feet.

"I . . ." she started, then stopped. She looked straight ahead. "I . . . Well, I haven't been very congenial, and I apologize. I know you're in pain and, well, I'm sorry I've been such a shrew."

What? she thought. For Pete's sake, what on earth was she saying? Hadn't she just had an in-depth conversation with herself regarding the necessity to keep a firm barrier between herself and Drew? Yes, she had.

And hadn't she determined that said wall was being constructed quite nicely by her acid tongue and lack of concern for Drew's injury? Yes, she had.

So why was she suddenly apologizing like a naughty child? She was crumbling her protective shield into dust with her own words. Good grief, she was an idiot.

"You're right," Drew said.

She snapped her head around to look at him, irrationally wondering if he'd read her mind.

"Pardon me?" she said.

"I'm simply agreeing with you," he said. "You've been a grouch, all right. The term 'coldhearted' comes to mind too. A broken wrist is not what I call having a rollicking fun time." He paused. "You have, as they say, an attitude problem."

She jumped to her feet. Dog followed suit.

"Well, excuse me to hell and back," she said. "Do recall, Mr. Sloan, that you're trespassing on private property, which does not produce the welcome wagon. I'm also stuck hauling you all the way into Tumbleweed—thirty-five-point-four miles, to be exact—to have your oh-so-terrible injury tended to. An injury, I might add, that would never have happened if you weren't out here in the wilds attempting to do something you have no idea how to do, even if you are wearing two-hundred-dollar hiking boots."

She took a gulp of much-needed air.

"I hereby retract my apology," she said, lifting her chin. "You're not only trespassing, you're also extremely rude."

"Me?" he said, his eyes widening. He pushed himself up, standing toe-to-toe with her. "*I'm* rude? Not even close, sweetheart. That title is yours in championship style. You're gorgeous, really beautiful, but . . . Ah, hell."

Before he fully realized he'd done it, Drew slid his left hand to the nape of her neck, lowered his head, and kissed her.

Her lips were as soft, as sweet, as he'd imagined. Kissing Memory was an explosion of senses like nothing he'd experienced before. She tasted like nectar and her special aroma filled him, a fragrance of flowers and fresh air and something so purely feminine, it was impossible to define. The soft skin of her neck felt like velvet beneath his work-roughened hand, and her hair glided like silk across it.

Heated, sensual sensations swept through him, and he was about to pull her closer when nature intervened. The dark clouds above them opened and heavy rain began to fall. Heavy, cold rain. Rain that soaked them both to the skin in moments, bringing them back to harsh reality. They stared at each other for a moment, then Memory's mouth tightened and eyebrows knitted together in a scowl Drew was beginning to recognize.

"That does it," she snapped, and spun around and marched off.

Drew followed, barely able to hear her muttering above the sound of the wind and torrential rain.

"I'm going to get pneumonia and die," she said, "because we had to stop to let his royal highness rest. What he is is a royal pain in the tush."

Drew smiled. For a moment he forgot the pain in

his arm and his soggy, cold clothes. For a moment he relived that kiss. He hadn't planned to kiss Memory, he'd just done it, and what a kiss it had been.

And as frosting on his fantastic cake, it was no longer necessary to imagine what was hidden beneath Memory's flannel shirt. That shirt was plastered to her like a second skin, sculpting the curve from her tiny waist to her nicely rounded hips.

Sensational.

However, as great as the view of Memory was now, he could no longer ignore the pain in his arm, the cold, driving rain, and the chilled-to-the-bone state of his body.

Memory's next words confirmed she was no happier.

"I'm freezing!" she raised her voice to be heard above the storm. "I should have been paying closer attention to those clouds. April weather is very unpredictable up here. I've seen spring flowers blossom one day, then the next day it snows." She glanced at the German shepherd trotting along in front of her. "Oh, well, Dog loves the rain, so at least someone is happy. Right, Dog?"

Dog's tail was wagging and he barked once as though to confirm everything she had said. Memory glanced back at Drew, smiling, and he instantly smiled in return. Quickly she looked ahead again, concentrating on her footing.

That rotten bum, she thought. No man should

have a smile like that. Nor should any man be able to turn her insides upside down with a simple kiss. She should have slapped him for being so presumptuous, but if she had, she would have been a hypocrite. She had enjoyed that kiss just as much as she believed he had, and that really frightened her. Men like him were not supposed to pop up out of nowhere on her mountain. This was her haven, her safe place, and Drew did *not* belong there. Damn him.

"Hey," he yelled suddenly. "How much farther do we have to go to get to . . . Oh, that's great. I don't even know where we're going. If you're lost, Memory Lawson, you might as well confess right now. A little more bad news won't make this day any worse than it already is."

She stopped and turned to face him, the shotgun cradled in her arms like a baby. Dog turned, too, tongue hanging out, tail wagging.

"I am not lost, Sloan." Her words were slow and measured, fury ringing in each one. "I know every inch of this land as well as I know my own name. I was born here. I've lived right here my entire life, except for when I . . ."

Her voice trailed off. She averted her eyes from his as she swept the rain from her face with a jerky motion of one hand.

Drew closed the distance between them to stand directly in front of her. He was vaguely aware that the rain had slackened and was a steady, quieter fall.

"Well, that's comforting," he said. "At least I know we're not lost. But you've got me curious now. You've lived here all your life except for when . . . When what?"

"It's not important," she said, looking at a spot over his right shoulder. "I was simply making the point that it would be impossible for me to get lost on this land."

He nodded. "Right, because you've been here for twenty-six years, except for when you . . . Are you going to leave me to fill in that blank with my imagination? I could come up with some real beauts.

"Let's see . . . Except for when you were leading safaris in deepest Africa, or when you were a cat burglar ripping off the rich in Paris, or when—"

She interrupted him with a laugh. "I think you broke your wrist *and* your brain."

He stared at her, his expression serious. "Memory, your laughter is one of the loveliest sounds I've ever heard. It's really—"

"Drew, could we cut the chitchat? We don't have far to go, and it's ridiculous to stand here in the rain talking nonsense." She spun around. "Let's get going."

She was a grouch again, Drew thought, following her. But nothing would erase from his mind the remembrance of her laughter, or the taste and feel of her lips.

Five minutes later, as the rain tapered off to a drizzle, they arrived at the bottom of Memory

Mountain. Memory led him through a dense grouping of tall pine trees. On the other side of the pines, lush, flat land stretched before them. Beyond a field of thick grass was a house, a welcoming sight with smoke curling up from two chimneys.

"Nice place," Drew said, as they came closer. "It's very . . . ranchy. What I mean is, it fits in perfectly here. The barn back there and the corrals are a nice touch. It really looks like a ranch out of the Old West."

"Drew," Memory said, "it *is* a ranch, a working ranch, right here in the present West. It is *my* ranch, and I run it."

"You're kidding. You're in charge of this operation? What do you grow or . . . well, whatever a person does on a ranch these days."

"Horses. I raise some of the finest horses in Arizona."

"That's really something, Memory," he said, nodding. "I'm impressed."

"You should be," she said, unable to hide her smile. "I'm very good at what I do."

"I'm sure you are. You must . . . um, spend a lot of time outside. You certainly handle yourself well on rough terrain, and you obviously ride. Do you ever go camping?"

"Yes, when the fish are biting. There's nothing like the taste of freshly caught fish that have been cooked over a mesquite fire."

"You've got *that* straight," he said. "'Delicious' isn't a good enough word to describe it."

"Oh?" She looked at him in surprise. "There's a restaurant in wherever you're from that actually prepares fresh fish over a mesquite fire?"

"I'm from Santa Barbara and, no, I'm not talking about eating fish in a restaurant."

"Santa Barbara, California," she said musingly. "Ritzy city, to say the least, with lots of money and millionaires and celebrities. No, thank you, I'll pass."

"You sure are quick to label people, Memory, and all in the negative. Men act like whining little boys when they get hurt, Santa Barbara is the pits because of wealthy people. It's not really fair to categorize like that, you know."

She shrugged. "I have the right to my opinions. There's no law written that says they have to match yours, Sloan."

"I think you're very narrow-minded . . . Lawson."

"Fine. Well, here we are at last," she went on as they crossed the driveway in front of the house. "We'll walk around to the back and go in through the mud room. If we mess up Tina's floor, there'll be hell to pay."

"Who's Tina?"

"My housekeeper. She lives here."

As Drew followed Memory along the side of the house toward the rear, his gaze swept over her home. The one-story ranch house was large, made of red brick and with a shingle roof.

Very nice, he mused. The barn and other buildings in the distance were painted barn-red, and the multitude of corral fences were white. For someone who wrinkled her nose about the wealthy of Santa Barbara, Memory was obviously financially flush herself. A person didn't own a spread like this on loose change.

Memory pulled open the back door, and they stepped into a room about ten by twelve feet in size, with a concrete floor. One wall had three rows of pegs from which hung jackets, shirts, and Stetsons.

At the far end of the room was what appeared to be a stall shower. A table next to it held a stack of fluffy towels.

After shrugging off his backpack, Memory wiped her shotgun dry, then slid it into a rack that held another shotgun, as well as three rifles.

"That weapon of yours was really loaded, huh?" Drew asked.

"Oh, yes, I filled the cartridges myself, but not with buckshot."

"No?"

"Nope. I use rock salt."

"Rock salt." He frowned. "Rock salt?"

She turned to him, her hands on her hips, a smile on her face, and he nearly groaned aloud. It wasn't from the pain, which seemed to have spread to every inch of his body, but from the coil of heated desire that had instantly tightened in his body. He knew Memory had no idea what an enticing picture she presented as she stood there in her wet and clinging clothes. Her wild hair had been transformed into a sleek frame for her face, accentuating her enormous dark eyes and sensual lips.

He was vaguely aware of her explaining, with intermingled laughter, that if she'd aimed that shotgun at his backside and pulled the trigger, he'd have a new respect for rock salt.

Actually, what Drew had new respect for was the good Lord's wisdom in shaping a woman's body with such intriguing curves. By putting her hands on her hips, Memory had pulled her shirt tight over her full breasts, and Drew could barely keep from staring.

A man, he thought wryly, had really been thrown off kilter by a woman, when said man was actually *glad* he'd broken his wrist, so that he didn't have to leave the woman just yet.

Memory chattered on about rock salt not really injuring anyone, but that it stung like the dickens and could break the skin just enough to make sitting down a painful experience for a while.

Drew smiled vaguely and nodded, as though her dissertation on what she was now referring to as a new definition of "salt in the wound" was the most fascinating thing he'd ever heard.

In actuality he was giving his body firm directives to remain under his command. He was also wondering just what might develop between him and the beautiful Memory Lawson. Even simply standing next to her sent his libido rocketing. If he didn't kiss her again soon, he'd probably go straight out of his ever-lovin' mind.

"Rock salt," another voice said, snapping Drew back to attention. "I remember a young girl who got her bottom full of it when she raided Charlie Ferguson's apple orchard once too often."

A short, plump woman, who appeared to be in her early fifties, came into the room. She had salt-and-pepper hair worn in a bun at the nape of her neck, an olive complexion, and a big smile.

This, Drew decided, must be Tina.

"Yes, well," Memory said. She cleared her throat. "That was a long time ago. Tina Toricelli, meet Drew Sloan. Drew, this is my housekeeper, though that's only one of her numerous titles."

"Hello," Drew said.

"My pleasure," Tina said. "You two look like drowned rats. You know you have to watch the sky at this time of year, Memory."

"Of course I know that. Mr. Sloan was trespassing on Memory Mountain, Tina. He then proceeded to fall over his own backpack and break his wrist."

"Now wait a minute—" Drew began.

"So our trek here was slowed considerably," Memory went on, "by the fact that Drew had to rest."

"Hey!"

"Now we have to get dry," she continued, as though he hadn't spoken, "and I've got to drive him into Tumbleweed to have a cast put on his wrist."

"What an adventure," Tina said. "I suppose you threatened to shoot him with that shotgun of yours."

"Damn right she did," Drew said. "How was I supposed to know I was hiking on her private hill? She popped up out of nowhere with her big gun and killer dog."

Dog wagged his tail.

Tina rolled her eyes. "Squabble, squabble. You two sound like children on a playground. Memory, go shower and change. Drew, I'm going to splint your wrist and call my husband in from the barn to help you out of those wet clothes and into some of his dry ones. You're bigger than he is, but borrowers can't be choosy." She looked back at Memory. "You haven't moved. Go. Go."

"Oh," Memory said. "Right away." She hurried out of the room.

"Amazing," Drew said, watching her go. "She didn't argue with you."

"She knows better," Tina said, moving to a telephone on the wall. "I was here when she was born, and raised her myself since she was fourteen years old. She doesn't make a fuss with her Mama Tina." She lifted the receiver. "You'll do as I tell you, too, Drew Sloan, if you know what's good for you."

"Yes, ma'am," he said, nodding quickly.

"Fine."

• • •

In the bathroom off the master bedroom, Memory stood under the warm cascade of water in the shower and closed her eyes.

A wave of fatigue engulfed her and she sighed, yearning to crawl between the crisp sheets on her bed and sleep for days.

She wasn't physically tired, but was emotionally drained. The unexpected appearance of Drew Sloan on her mountain, and the unsettling effect he had on her, had produced a bone-deep weariness.

She opened her eyes to reach for the shampoo, and moments later was scrubbing her hair with more force than was necessary.

The old show tune wasn't true, she thought. Washing her hair wasn't going to rid herself of Drew. She still had to drive him all the way into Tumbleweed, wait while his wrist was X-rayed and a cast put on it, then . . .

"Then what?" she said aloud, causing her to swallow a mouthful of water.

She coughed and sputtered, then began to rinse the shampoo from her hair.

Well, dandy, she fumed. Drew wouldn't be able to manage a stick shift even after his wrist was tended to. She'd have to bring him back to the ranch, then allow him to stay until a friend or relative could come to his rescue.

Damn. She didn't want him there. He was just

too male, too handsome, too mesmerizing when he smiled that lethal smile.

And when he'd kissed her . . . She had thought she had buried her sensuality, her needs, six years earlier, yet after only a couple of hours with Drew, all of those desires were beginning to clamor within her.

She turned off the water with an angry jerk of the faucet, then dried herself with a large towel. As she blow-dried her hair, she gave herself a lecture.

Through her ranch business, she dealt with men continually. Those who made advances were quickly put in their place by an icy stare or a sharp retort that left no doubt in their minds that they were out of line.

She had a reputation for being an excellent horse breeder who was strictly business and not interested in any goings-on in the male-female arena.

So she just had to treat Drew the way she treated every other man who crossed her path. He was there, he'd soon be gone, and that would be that.

"Excellent," she said, leaving the bathroom.

Dressed in jeans, boots, and a bright red cable-knit sweater, she headed downstairs. When she entered the kitchen she stopped, her eyes widening as her gaze swept over Drew.

"My goodness," she said, "aren't you a fashion plate?" barely restraining a giggle. The jeans he wore ended just above the ankle, and the cuffs of the flannel shirt missed his wrist by a good four inches.

Drew glared at her in response.

"Drew is bigger than Franco," Tina said as she finished fastening a sling at the back of Drew's neck. "There you are, Drew. Your wrist is splinted, that sling will hold it still, and you've had two aspirin. That's the best we can do here. They'll fix you up properly in Tumbleweed."

"Thank you, Tina," Drew said, shooting Memory another dark look. "I appreciate your help, and Franco's clothes. You and your husband are very kind."

"What about me?" Memory asked. "I'm kind. I'm the one who's going to drive you into Tumbleweed, aren't I?"

"You are . . ." Drew stopped as he stared at her. She was sensational in that red sweater. What it did for her dark hair and eyes, and her peaches-and-cream complexion, was unbelievable. And there were those lips again. "You are . . ."

"I'm what?" she asked.

"Don't tease, Memory," Tina said. "Drew is in pain and does not, I'm sure, want to squabble with you anymore. Now then, you two sit down and have some pie and coffee. That will hold you until you can get back here for dinner."

"There's no time for a snack," Memory said. "The roads will be muddy from the rain, and I'll have to drive slowly."

"I'd love some pie and coffee," Drew said, sitting back in his chair at the table.

"Sloan," Memory said, narrowing her eyes, "you're pushing me."

"Lawson, I'm accepting Tina's *kind* offer of pie. She is a very *kind* lady. You ought to try being *kind* sometime. You might like it."

Tina laughed. "Drew, hush. Now *you're* stirring things up. Compromise is called for here. Have some pie, but don't dillydally while you're eating it."

"Mmm," Memory said, managing to make it sound grumpy. She sank onto a chair and drummed the fingers of one hand on the top of the table. "Mmm."

Within minutes Tina had set pie and coffee in front of them. Memory began eating, but Drew frowned down at the food.

"I'm right-handed," he said. "How am I going to eat this?"

"If you think I'm going to feed you, you're nuts," Memory said. "Pick up your fork, spear a chunk of pie, and aim for your mouth. Maybe you'll get lucky." She shrugged. "If the pie lands in your ear, you'd better call it quits."

"Mmm," Drew said, matching the tone she'd used. "You're flunking *kind* big-time, Memory."

"Hush, hush," Tina said, laughing. "You two are something."

As Drew attempted to maneuver a forkful of pie

to his mouth with his left hand, Memory snuck glances at him from beneath her lashes.

It was taking every bit of willpower she had not to reach across the table, take the fork from his hand, and feed him. In her mind's eye, she could see his lips closing over the bite of pie, his gaze riveted to hers the entire time. The scenario was strangely erotic, extremely provocative.

A shiver coursed through Memory, and she jabbed her fork into her pie, nearly causing the pastry to slide off the plate.

There was nothing attractive, she told herself firmly, about a man dressed in clothes that were ridiculously too small. But Drew was so pale, despite his tan. He was being a real trouper about the pain she knew he was suffering, and was struggling like a little boy to accomplish a difficult task.

He looked vulnerable and sweet, like someone who needed a comforting hug, and she'd love to jump up and volunteer for the job.

Memory, stop it, she admonished herself. She'd taken herself in hand and regained control. She was going to ignore the funny flutter in the pit of her stomach, and the heat thrumming low within her. Right now. *Control, Memory Lawson, control.*

The silence in the kitchen was broken by the sound of a door slamming. Memory set down her fork and quickly stood up. Drew looked questioningly at her, then a moment later his eyes widened in shock.

A little girl dashed into the room, her dark eyes sparkling, long black braids flying.

"Heather," Memory said, opening her arms. "Hello, sweetheart."

The child flung herself into Memory's embrace, and Drew stared at the pair, his fork still held in midair.

"Hi, Mommy," Heather said. "I'm home from school. Can I have some pie?"

Three

Silence prevailed in the cab of the pickup truck as Memory drove slowly along the muddy unpaved road. Neither she nor Drew had spoken in the fifteen minutes since they'd left the ranch.

Drew slid yet another glance at her, then turned his head to stare out the side window.

He could literally feel the wall that she had erected between them in that truck. The closed expression on her face, the rigid set to her shoulders and back, her tight grip on the steering wheel, all shouted the message that she was to be left alone.

Well, tough, he thought. If he wanted to talk, he'd talk. And he *did* want to talk. What did Memory expect him to do? Pretend that little Heather hadn't appeared in the kitchen announcing to her "Mommy" that she was home from school?

A strange lump had formed in Drew's throat when he'd seen the soft, loving expression on Memory's face as she'd swung her daughter up into her arms.

After setting the girl down, Memory had introduced Heather to Drew, carefully keeping her gaze from meeting his. The little girl had looked him over, asked if he had a boo-boo on his arm, and told him she was five years old. She'd finished off the job of capturing his heart by telling him that it was okay if he wanted to cry if his broken bone hurt really, really bad.

Tina had produced pie for Heather, along with milk in a mug that boasted a picture of Minnie and Mickey Mouse.

Memory had bustled around, taking her dirty dishes to the sink, gathering jackets, and chattering to Heather about a trip to Tumbleweed being in order so that Dr. Sanchez could fix Drew's wrist, that Heather should change out of her school dress, be a good girl for Tina, and Mommy would be back in time for dinner.

Now, there they were, Drew thought, Memory and he in Silent City, acting as though she'd just picked him up along the side of the road and had a policy of not speaking to strangers. Well, the heck with his nonsense.

He turned, looking at Memory again. "Heather sure is cute."

"Oh, Lord," Memory said, flicking him a quick glance. "You startled me."

"Were you sleeping?" he asked, raising his eyebrows. "It's been so quiet in here, you could easily have dozed off. As I was saying, your daughter is a nifty little kid."

"Thank you."

"She sure takes after you," he went on. "She's a pint-size image of you."

"Yes, I know. People have remarked on that quite frequently."

"Where does Heather go to school?"

"School? Oh, there's state land about five miles from the ranch. The school is there, and they pick her up in a bus. I went there when I was growing up. Heather attends afternoon kindergarten this year."

"Oh, yeah? So, next year is first grade. I bet you'll miss her when she's gone all day."

"Yes," Memory said quietly. "Yes, I will. She's . . . well, she's my sunshine."

Drew nodded. "I like the way you said that. It's true, too. I can easily see where she'd brighten the gloomiest day. Yep, Heather Lawson is a smile waiting to happen."

Memory's head snapped around and she looked at Drew, then quickly redirected her attention to the road as the truck hit a pothole.

"What makes you think her last name is Lawson?"

He shrugged. "Your last name is Lawson. Dur-

ing one of your screamers up on your mountain,
you announced that you'd never been, nor did you
ever intend to be, married." He shrugged again.
"Elementary. Her name is Heather Lawson."

"Oh. Well, yes, I guess I did say that about
marriage. It's no secret around here that Heather
doesn't have a father. No one thinks twice about
it. She's my daughter and she's totally accepted as
such."

Drew didn't miss the edge in her voice. "You're
awfully defensive about it, Memory. You sound
like you're daring me to press the issue. You didn't
marry Heather's father. Okay, fine. That's really
nobody's business but yours."

"But you can't help wondering—"

"Dammit, Memory," he interrupted, surprising
himself with his sudden flash of anger, "would
you lighten up? What is it with you? It seems as
though you're always looking for a fight. You're
ready to go ten rounds at the drop of a hat."

She opened her mouth to retort, her dark eyes
sparkling with anger as she glanced at him.

"No, don't say anything," he said, raising his left
hand in a halting gesture. "Just listen a minute."
He paused, and his tone was gentle when he
spoke again. "Memory, I'm not stupid. Okay? The
minute that Heather came flying into the kitchen
and called you Mommy, I put it together with what
you'd said earlier about never having been married."

"Mmm," she said, frowning.

"Hush. My first, last, and only thought when I realized you were an unwed mother was that if your situation meant that there was a man out there somewhere who had hurt you, I'd like to find him and take him apart."

She blinked. "Pardon me?"

"You heard me. That's the truth, Memory. It was my gut reaction, and it hasn't changed."

"Oh."

Oh, dear, Memory thought. Oh, darn. She was acutely aware of unexpected and definitely unwelcomed tears prickling at the back of her eyes. She knew, just somehow knew, that Drew was being honest about his feelings regarding Heather.

Blast it, what was she supposed to do with what he had said? There was no room in her protective wall for such a thing as a sweet, nonjudgmental, knight in shining armor who was ready to slay the dragons.

"Do you believe me?" he asked.

She nodded, not attempting to speak past the lump in her throat.

"Good."

She looked over at him and their eyes met, just for a moment. But during that tick of time, that one heartbeat, something changed. They somehow moved into a place of greater understanding, communication, accompanied by a smattering of trust that brought with it a warm, comforting glow.

Memory Lawson was frightened to the very depths of her soul.

Drew Sloan felt the greatest joy he had ever known.

"Good," he repeated, and settled into a more comfortable position, making no attempt to hide the smile on his face.

During the remaining miles to Tumbleweed, no further words were spoken.

Tumbleweed, Arizona, was not cute, pretty, or quaint. It was simply there, a block long, and consisting of a café, a gas station, a general store with the post office substation tucked into one corner, and a laundromat.

The clinic was in a storefront that had, years before, housed a shoe repair shop. Financed by a government grant, it was run by Dr. Rick Sanchez, a tall, good-looking man in his early thirties, who was of Mexican-American descent.

It took exactly six seconds for Drew to decide that he didn't like Sanchez. The doctor's face had lit up like fireworks on the Fourth of July when Memory walked into the clinic. His teeth—revealed by his broad smile—had to be capped, Drew thought, because no one had teeth that perfect. And was it really necessary for randy Rick to stand so damn close to Memory?

After Memory had made the appropriate introductions and explained what had happened to Drew, Sanchez turned to him.

"Are you married?" Drew asked bluntly.

Rick raised his eyebrows in surprise.

"Married?" he repeated. "No. Are you?"

"No."

"What," Memory asked, "does the fact that no one in this room is married have to do with Drew's wrist?"

"Nothing," the two men said in unison.

"Men are weird," she muttered.

Drew and Rick stared at each other for a long moment in the age-old ritual of males sizing one another up. Then Rick began to remove the splint.

"Hey," Drew said, "take it easy. That's a broken bone you're dealing with, Sanchez."

"I'm aware of that, Sloan. I'm a doctor, remember? What do *you* do for a living?"

"I'm part owner of Sloan Nursery and Landscaping."

"Oh, really?" Memory said. "That sounds fascinating. Drew's from Santa Barbara, Rick."

Rick smiled. "Oh? Just passing through, huh? That's nice."

"My 'passing,'" Drew said, "has been delayed. I can't exactly drive a vehicle with a standard transmission. Right, Doc?"

"The airplane has been invented," Rick said.

Memory sighed impatiently. "This is all very fascinating chitchat, but could we get on with it here? I'd like to get back to the ranch before it starts to rain again. The roads are bad enough as it is."

"You bet," Drew said. "Don't you fret, Memory. We'll be home in time to have dinner with Heather."

"Step over there to the X-ray machine," Rick said.

As the two men crossed the room, Memory watched them go, her head cocked, eyebrows knitted in concentration.

Some strange, tense vibes were zinging back and forth between Drew and Rick. What their problem was, she couldn't fathom. But then, she'd never claimed to be able to understand men's minds, nor did she care to. But then again . . . Oh, forget it.

She sank onto an orange plastic chair and picked up a year-old copy of *Field and Stream*. As she leafed idly through it, a niggling voice whispered in her head, a voice that steadily gained volume until she could no longer ignore what it was repeating.

We'll be home in time to have dinner with Heather.
We'll be home in time to have dinner with Heather.
We'll be home—

Stop, Memory silently demanded, pressing her fingertips to her temples. Drew hadn't meant that as intimately as it had sounded. He'd simply chosen common words into which she was reading far too much.

For all she knew, his statement was related to

the unexplainable whatever-it-was that was crackling through the air between Drew and Rick.

We'll be home in time to have dinner with Heather.

Darn it, Memory thought, why did those words insist on echoing in her mind? And why did they create a warm feeling deep within her?

It was as though a tiny gremlin was dancing around in her brain with a paintbrush, creating vivid mental pictures. She could clearly see herself, Heather, and Drew sitting at the kitchen table eating dinner. They were laughing, talking, sharing. They were a family.

Oh, Memory, she admonished herself, don't. Why her mind was traveling down this road, she didn't know. Years before, she'd vowed to be both mother and father to Heather, and she was doing just fine. She didn't want, nor need, a man in her life. Not ever again.

"Well, there we go," Rick said. "One old-fashioned soggy plaster-of-paris cast. We don't have the fancy new kind here that dries in a flash and can waltz right into the shower with you. Next time you break something, Sloan, try doing it closer to a big city."

"I'll keep that in mind," Drew said.

"Stay put for twenty minutes so that can set," Rick went on. "It won't dry completely for two days, so you'll have to wear a sling during the next forty-eight hours. Through the six weeks the cast is on, don't get it wet. Cover it with a plastic trash bag when you take a shower. I'll give you some

pain pills in case you have trouble sleeping tonight. That wrist is liable to throb like a nasty
toothache for a while. Any questions?"

"Am I having fun yet?" Drew asked, smiling
slightly.

Rick laughed. "Hey, yeah. A broken bone is a
thrill a minute."

Memory got to her feet and crossed the room,
wrinkling her nose as she looked at Drew's arm
and the general mess on the table.

"Yuck," she said.

"I'd better wash up," Rick said, turning to the
sink.

"Well, lesson learned, Drew," Memory said. "You
shouldn't tackle something that you're not properly trained to do."

Drew frowned. "What are you talking about?"

"Hiking. There's a lot more to it than getting
expensive boots and matching jacket and sweatshirt. I'm sure you realize that by now."

"This," he said, pointing to the cast, "was a
fluke, a freak accident. I'll have you know, Miss
Memory Mountain, that I've been hiking, camping,
riding the rapids, the whole nine yards, for more
years than I can remember. I don't know where you
got the idea I'm an armchair-quarterback type of
outdoorsman, but you're wrong. In fact, this accident wouldn't have happened if you hadn't been
playing Annie Oakley with your big shotgun."

Memory pressed one hand to her chest. "Now

it's all *my* fault? That figures." She folded her arms and lifted her chin. "Men are such dolts."

"Thanks a lot," Rick said, scrubbing the table with a sponge. "You're not about to launch into one of your 'All men are . . .' sermons, are you? It really bugs me when you do that."

Drew looked over at Rick. "You've got that straight. She's laid a few of those on me already. It's irritating as hell."

Rick nodded. "I, personally, am a very nice guy. I don't deserve being lumped in with a group of yo-yos."

"Exactly," Drew said. "And I resent being told I don't know squat about hiking. Just because I'm from the city, she figures I'm playing at this. She jumps to conclusions about people, you know."

Rick nodded, continuing to scrub the table. "Then there's the topic she gets off on about how men—"

"Would you two just shut up?" Memory yelled. Drew and Rick stared at her. "Stop talking about me as though I weren't here. That's extremely rude."

"And I suppose all men are rude," Drew said, his own voice rising.

"The two I'm looking at certainly are. I'll be waiting in the truck. When your show-and-tell plaster of paris sets enough to move it, haul yourself outside. I refuse to stand here another moment and be insulted." She spun around. "Good-bye."

The two men watched her stomp across the

room, and both cringed when she slammed the door behind her.

"A bit ticked," Rick said.

"More than a bit," Drew said. "She's really something, isn't she? Those were laser beams shooting from her eyes. When her temper gets in a rip, she's dynamite." He stared at the closed door. "I've never met anyone like Memory Lawson before."

"Memory is very unique," Rick said quietly. "I don't know where you think you're headed with her, Sloan, but listen up. If you hurt her, you'll answer to me."

Drew turned to look at Rick. "Are you in love with her?"

Rick sighed. "Hell, I don't know. I'm not certain I'd recognize love if it popped me in the chops. What I *am* certain of is that Memory is special, within herself and to me. I won't stand by and see her become the victim of a heartless game."

"I wouldn't do that."

"Then we understand each other. You've got about five more minutes, then I'll put a sling on you and you can go."

"How much do I owe you?"

"I'll write you up a bill right now. This clinic is operating on a shoestring, so I'm going to charge you plenty for this little visit."

"Go for it. Sanchez . . . Rick, Tina said something about having raised Memory since Memory was fourteen. What happened to her parents?"

"I wasn't here then, and Memory has never talked about it much. I asked her once, and she said they died. That's all . . . they died. I could tell from the way she said it that the subject was closed to discussion."

"So you don't know how they died?"

"Actually, I do. It's no secret around here. They were killed in a small-plane crash. I've heard only good things about her folks. They were very well thought of, highly respected. Losing them had to have been devastating to a fourteen-year-old girl. To this day, Memory simply won't talk about it."

Drew nodded. "What about Heather?"

"She's a heart stealer, isn't she? She's a great kid. But Heather is another subject Memory won't discuss. We've shared a lot, Memory and I, but those two topics are off-limits. I'd been here about three months when I first met Memory. She'd been away several years, then showed up with a brand new baby girl. She literally dared anyone to make a fuss about it, and no one did. Memory was welcomed back home and her daughter was accepted, no questions asked."

"Memory runs that big ranch herself?"

"Well, Franco is there, and quite a few hands. Franco and Tina kept the place going during the few years Memory was away." Rick looked at Drew's cast. "Okay, let's get a sling on you. Memory is probably out in that truck fuming. Drew, I have a feeling you're in for a stone-cold silent drive back to the ranch."

"No joke," he said. "That one, Rick, you can take all the way to the bank."

The drive back to the ranch was made in stone-cold silence.

There were times, Drew thought as they parked by the side of the house, that he'd prefer to be wrong.

"Give me the keys to your vehicle," Memory said, turning off the ignition. "Tell me where it is, and I'll have a couple of the boys go get it." She opened the door of the truck and got out.

Drew shifted until he was able to open his door with his left hand and met Memory at the side of the truck. He gave her his keys and explained where he'd parked his vehicle.

"All right," she said. "I'll go down to the barn and see who's free."

"Memory," he said as she turned away.

"Yes?" She met his gaze for the first time since they'd left Tumbleweed.

"Thank you for taking me to the clinic. I appreciate it very much. I'll call my brothers and see if one of them can get away from the nursery long enough to come over here. If that plan fizzles, I'll think of something else. I'll be out of here as quickly as possible, because I realize my hanging around is an imposition."

"Oh, well, I . . ."

"Do you have a bunkhouse, or whatever you call

it, where your hands sleep? I could bed down there for the night."

"Yes, there's a bunkhouse, but the beds are narrow. You'll need to prop your arm on pillows tonight, which will be much more comfortable than having it on your chest. You can sleep in the house. One of the spare rooms has a double bed."

"Thank you."

"No problem."

"Memory, look, I realize that Rick and I ticked you off, but we didn't mean to. I apologize if we offended you. It wasn't our intention, believe me."

She sighed. "I know. I—I overreacted and threw a tantrum. I'm the one who should apologize, and I do. Go on into the house. I'll be in later."

Drew made no move toward the house as he watched her walk away.

Memory drew a deep, steadying breath as she headed for the barn, then frowned in disgust.

She'd been an idiot again, she told herself. She should have shuffled Drew off to eat and sleep with the hands. But oh, no, not Mindless Memory. She'd insisted that he eat at her table and sleep under her roof.

She'd had to actually bite her tongue to keep from blithering on that there was no rush for him to leave. There was, after all, plenty of room in the house and goodness, no, his staying wasn't an imposition.

She'd stood there by the truck, making the mistake, again, of looking into Drew Sloan's mesmerizing eyes. Her heart had skipped a beat, and she'd been aware of that now familiar heat curling deep within her. As she'd gazed at him, she'd felt overwhelmed by his blatant masculinity, even as her own femininity rose within her, as if in answer to a silent call.

Dear heaven, she had to send him away as quickly as possible.

"Memory, wait up," he called.

She jerked to a stop and turned to see him striding toward her, holding his injured arm secure against his chest.

"Yes?" she asked when he stopped in front of her.

"I thought I'd tag along, see some more of your operation here."

"Now?"

"Sure. Why not?"

"Whatever," she said, and started off again.

He fell into step beside her. "What's that small barn over there for? It looks like a scaled-down version of the big one. Is it a playhouse for Heather?"

"No. Heather has strict instructions never to go near there. It may look like a playhouse, but it's actually a heavily reinforced box stall where Thunder, my stallion, is kept. When there's a mare in season on the ranch, it takes two people with lead ropes to handle him."

"Oh, I see."

Up ahead, they saw a cowboy come out of the barn and wave to Memory. "Mr. Gladstone is on the phone," he said, jogging toward them. "This is the third time he's called in the past couple of hours. He's getting hot under the collar, says you were expecting his call to schedule when he can bring his mare from Kentucky to be bred with Thunder."

"Oh, damn," she said. "I completely forgot about it. Don't worry about it, Joe. Gladstone just has a short fuse. I'll go placate him." Without even looking at Drew, she hurried to the barn.

Drew frowned as he watched her disappear inside, then met Joe's gaze.

"This is my fault," he said. "Memory was in Tumbleweed because I needed to get my wrist set."

"Yep, you've banged yourself up, all right. Fall off a horse?"

"No, I . . . No."

"It's not like Memory to forget something as important as a call coming through from Gladstone. The man thinks he's got the finest mares ever born, and he deals only with Memory. He's a pain, but he puts out a lot of money in stud fees over a year's time. Well, I've got work to do. See ya."

"Right."

Drew paced restlessly as he waited for Memory to reappear. When she finally emerged from the barn, he strode over to meet her.

"Did you calm the guy down?" he asked.

"Yes. Gladstone is full of hot air, but he's worth keeping happy."

"I'm sorry, Memory. This wouldn't have happened if you hadn't taken me to Tumbleweed."

"I'm responsible for remembering important things like that call. It has nothing to do with you."

"Yes it does."

She frowned. "Oh, I see. It's easy for you to be noble now that you know the situation is under control. I'm sure you'd have a different song to sing if I'd said Gladstone had canceled bringing his mare in."

"Hey, now wait a minute—"

"Yes," she went on as if he hadn't spoken, "that would be par for a male-logic course. You'd say it wasn't your fault because how could you know I was expecting that call."

"Dammit, Memory, that's not fair. You've decided I'd let *you* take the blame if the deal with Gladstone had fallen through."

"Got it in one, Sloan."

"You're wrong, Lawson."

"Forget it," she said. "I've got to see about a feed order that's late, check on the pregnant mares, and write down the work schedule for tomorrow. Drew, please, just go on up to the house and let me tend to my chores."

He opened his mouth to deliver an angry retort, then snapped it closed again. When he turned and started toward the house, his jaw was set in a hard line of determination.

An hour later Memory entered the house through the mud room and slipped off her leather boots. As she padded into the kitchen in her stocking feet, she heard the glorious sound of Heather's laughter dancing through the air.

She glanced over to where Tina was cooking at the stove, and they exchanged smiles.

"Such a happy little girl," Tina said.

"Yes. That's a beautiful sound, isn't it? A child's laughter is prettier than words can describe."

"Angels singing. Go on into the living room, Memory, and relax. I'll call you when dinner is ready. With Drew here, do you want me to set places in the dining room?"

"Oh, no, that's not necessary. Drew is—" "Family," she'd almost said, to her horror. "What I mean is, Drew is just as comfortable as we are in the kitchen."

She started across the kitchen, then stopped, looking at Tina again.

"What you said a moment ago about angels. I think I remember . . . Yes, I *do* remember. I was about Heather's age, and I was crying in my room. Heaven only knows what I was upset about. My mother came in, picked me up, and nestled me on her lap."

Memory smiled as she relived the precious memory.

"She said to go ahead and cry, but then I was to smile and laugh, because the angels were waiting. When anyone laughs because they're happy, she said, the angels sing. When someone cries, the angels are sad."

Tina nodded.

"My mother told me," Memory went on quietly, "not to use laughter or tears lightly, to look into my heart to be certain each was real, because what I did made the difference between angels singing, angels sad."

"Yes," Tina said. "You've remembered it perfectly. She told you that many times."

"Angels singing, angels sad," Memory whispered. "That is so lovely."

"Yes, and you're never too old to put that beautiful thought to use. Now, go kiss Heather, then put your feet up a bit before dinner."

Memory gave the housekeeper a hug, then hurried from the room. Tina turned back to the stove, humming.

When Memory reached the archway to the living room, she stopped, her heart quickening as she drank in the scene before her.

A welcoming fire blazed in the huge flagstone fireplace, casting a rosy glow over Drew and

Heather, who sat together on the oatmeal-colored sofa.

Heather's eyes were sparkling as she stared up at Drew, an expression of rapt attention on her face.

"He was not," she said, and giggled.

"Oh, but he was, Honey Heather," Drew said, eyes wide with exaggerated sincerity. "That seven-foot-tall bear was wearing a red top hat, a red coat, and the snazziest bright red high-top tennies you ever saw. He came stomping up to where I was fishing and told me to get my pole out of *his* stream, because those were *his* fish, and no city slickers were allowed on *his* land."

"My mommy doesn't like people on her mountain or on her land neither," Heather said. "But she's a mommy, not a bear."

"Very true," Drew said, nodding. "She's a very beautiful mommy, as a matter of fact. You look just like her, so that makes you a very beautiful Honey Heather."

She digested that theory, then decided it made sense. "Yep."

"So, anyway," Drew went on, "I was really scared of that bear. He was so-o-o big and so-o-o crabby, and I was figuring he might gobble me up for lunch."

Heather dissolved in a fit of laughter, wrapping her arms around her tummy.

Angels singing, Memory thought, smiling. They were so dear together, Drew and Heather. Their rapport had been instant and honest. Heather was obviously enthralled with Drew, and he was focusing entirely on her, despite his grueling day and the pain she knew he must still be feeling.

What a wonderful father he would be, she mused. His sharing with Heather was true, and rich, and precious. He really should have a wife and children, a family.

We'll be home in time to have dinner with Heather.

His words thundered once again in her mind, and she shook her head as though to make them disappear. As the words continued to echo relentlessly, she forced herself to shift her attention back to Drew's story about the bear.

"'Well, I don't know,' the bear rumbled," Drew was saying. "'Why should I let you have any of my fish?' 'Mr. Bear,' I told him, 'look at these fine fish I've already caught. I'll cook them up over a mesquite fire, and we'll have us a mighty good meal. Then I'll go away, and not step foot again on your private land, unless you personally invite me to.'"

"What he say, what he say?" Heather asked, leaning toward Drew. "Did he want to keep all the fish just for hisself?"

"No, ma'am. He thought for a while, and I waited. Oh, I was shaking, wondering what was ticking away in that big bear brain of his. Then finally he said he'd agree to the plan, because it would be nice to have someone to talk with over a meal for a change. And do you know what I realized right then, Honey Heather?"

"What? What?"

"I knew that the bear was lonely. Oh, he didn't want anyone to find that out, you understand, but I could tell. He'd always stomped around, roaring, wearing his fancy clothes and telling folks to stay clear of his land, but in his heart he was a lonely bear."

"Oh," Heather said, wonder evident in her voice. "Poor, poor bear. He was sad."

"Yep. We had a fine supper of those fish, and we talked for a long time about all kinds of things, then I went on my way. Do you know what this story means?"

"Don't think so."

"Well, it's saying that it's fine to be able to take care of yourself and protect what's yours. But no one, not big bears with snazzy red tennies and not people, should forget that if you never let folks get close to you, walk in your space and share your dinner, you're going to be very, very lonely."

Heather slowly nodded, indicating that she understood the theme of Drew's tale.

Hot tears burned Memory's eyes as she stumbled backward, out of the archway and into the hall. She hurried to her bedroom and rushed inside, closing the door and leaning against it. The tears spilled onto her cheeks, and a sob caught in her throat.

Dammit, Memory, she inwardly fumed, dashing

the tears from her cheeks. Drew hadn't been delivering a message to her; he hadn't even known she was there. He'd simply made up a story for a little girl about a bear.

A lonely bear . . . a sad bear . . . a bear who kept everyone away from his land and far from his heart.

Just as she did.

But, no, no, she thought frantically, *she* wasn't lonely, she was perfectly fine. Her life was set up exactly the way she wanted it. It was ridiculous, overreacting like this to a story about a silly bear in red tennies.

As fresh tears filled her eyes, though, a devastating chill swept through her, touching her heart, the very essence of who she was, with clawing fingers.

Memory dropped her face into her trembling hands and wept.

Angels *singing?* her heart whispered. No, *angels sad.*

Four

Drew took a deep breath of the crisp night air and exhaled slowly. Resting his back against the house, he looked up at the star-filled sky. It looked like a multitude of exquisite, sparkling diamonds displayed against black velvet, he thought, and smiled.

The smile faded, though, as troubling thoughts pushed aside the serenity of the night. Something was wrong with Memory.

On the surface, she had appeared fine that evening. She'd chattered away at dinner, smiled and laughed with Heather, listened attentively while the little girl shared the adventures of her afternoon at school.

Still, Drew had sensed that something wasn't right with Memory. Her smile hadn't quite reached her eyes. Her laughter had been hollow and forced.

When she'd first appeared in the kitchen for dinner, her eyes had been puffy and slightly red. His inquiry as to why had been breezily dismissed as a sudden attack of allergies. There was no reason, he supposed, to doubt her explanation, but he hadn't believed it. He'd bet the farm that Memory had been crying.

Why?

Damn, he thought, shifting to a more comfortable position. He really hated the idea that she'd gone to her room after their return from Tumbleweed and cried. He'd apologized for the fact that he and Rick had acted like jerks. No, that dumb incident in the clinic wasn't enough to upset her that much.

Then what was it?

He didn't know.

He felt as though her sorrow were his as well. A bond had been forged between them on the mountain. He wanted to charge to the rescue, demand to know what had caused her tears, then fix whatever it was.

"Right," he muttered aloud.

He had wanted to talk to Memory, to find out what was distressing her, but that plan had fizzled. When she'd reappeared in the kitchen after tucking Heather in for the night, she'd announced that she had paperwork to tend to in her office.

He'd waited in the living room for over an hour, then given up and wandered outside. He could go to bed, he supposed, but his arm was throbbing.

Sleep would be impossible unless he took one of the pain pills that Rick Sanchez had given him, a solution that held no appeal. His brothers and sister teased him for being a health food nut, and maybe he did go overboard sometimes. Still, he objected to drugs of any sort.

His head snapped around as the door to the mud room was opened, and Memory stepped out of the house.

"Did you finish your paperwork?" he asked.

"It's never finished," she said, walking slowly toward him. "I'm caught up to an acceptable point."

She stopped next to him and leaned back as he was doing. Drew searched his mind for a way to ask what was upsetting her, but came up with a frustrating blank.

"Drew," she said, not looking at him. "I heard you telling Heather the story about the bear."

He turned toward her, propping one shoulder against the house. "Did you? I didn't know you were there."

"I realize that." She turned her head to meet his gaze, the soft light from the windows making it possible for them to see each other. "Why did you tell her that story? She obviously enjoyed it, and she understood it, but I can't help but wonder why you chose it."

Drew hesitated. He stared down at the ground for a long moment, before looking at Memory again.

"It's sort of complicated," he said in a low voice. "And, well, personal. The bear . . . the bear is me." He paused and cleared his throat. "Okay, I might as well tell you all of it. You see, I have two overachiever brothers, one older, one younger. They've always excelled at everything they've ever done. In school, they went out for sports and made the varsity team every time. The honor roll was a given for them and they hardly ever cracked a book." He smiled briefly. "I wasn't quite so fortunate. Lord knows I love them, but it's pretty rough growing up and being aware that you're always falling short."

"Did they realize how you felt?"

"No, not really, because they weren't intentionally trying to show me up. Anyway, I stepped out of their shadows by pursuing something that didn't interest them, that is, hiking, camping, fishing, all kinds of outdoor activities."

Memory nodded.

"The problem was," he continued, "that my separateness, if you want to call it that, began to spread into other areas of my life without my being aware it was happening. I started keeping everyone at arm's length, existing in a world of my own, with all my own interests and where no one was allowed to get too close.

"After I graduated from college and started working at Sloan Nursery and Landscaping full-time, I had to face the distance between myself and my family, day after day. I also had to face the fact that I was a very lonely man."

"The bear," she said softly.

"Yes, just like the sad, lonely bear in my story. I'm just grateful that I realized what I'd done before it was too late."

Oh, Drew, Memory thought. What had it cost him to reveal all of that to her? She had been given a gift, a deeper, richer understanding of who Drew Sloan really was.

She wanted to wrap her arms around him in a comforting embrace, tell him that his story of the bear had touched something within her too.

She wouldn't reach out to him, though, nor comment further on what he'd revealed. If she did, he might misinterpret her words and actions, view them as her reacting and responding to him on a sexual, emotional plane.

That wasn't the case, of course, she told herself. It was simply a matter of one human being recognizing the momentary vulnerable state of another human being.

"Actually," he said, pulling her from her thoughts, "I'm glad those few years took place, because when I recognized my mistake and made amends, my relationship with my family was better than ever, the bonds even stronger. I also found myself giving my maximum effort to Sloan Nursery and thoroughly enjoying it.

"We do some strange things to ourselves sometimes, Memory. I was lucky enough to have had a chance to retrace my steps and repair the damage." He looked at her intently. "Why did you ask about the bear?"

She shrugged. "No particular reason, other than curiosity. It wasn't a standard once-upon-a-time tale, and I'd wondered if you'd made it up and why you'd chosen to tell it to Heather. Thank you for sharing what you just did."

"I've never told anyone else. No one."

"Well, I'm honored," she said, attempting a smile that failed. Honored? she thought. How about deeply touched, close to bursting into tears? No. Any other emotions rising within her were due to its having been a long, exhausting day. "I think I'll say good night now, Drew. I'm very tired."

Drew barely restrained himself from reaching out to her. He wanted to pull her to him, hold her, kiss her, savor her taste, aroma, and the softness of her body nestled against him. This wasn't the time, however, though he wasn't certain how he knew that. Perhaps it was the lingering remembrance of dinner, when he'd been so acutely aware of her distress. And the fact that he still didn't know what had caused her to cry.

"Good night," he said quietly.

She turned and started toward the door.

"Memory?"

She stopped, but didn't look at him. "Yes?"

"Bears in red tennies come in all sizes, shapes, and ages. And sometimes, Memory, they're girl bears."

She stood perfectly still for another moment, then walked into the house.

Drew stared up at a ceiling he couldn't see in the dark bedroom. It was just after midnight and he had yet to even doze. He was rapidly approaching the point where he would swallow one of the pain pills with a sigh of relief, for the ache in his arm seemed to worsen with every second that passed.

"I give up," he said at last, swinging his feet to the floor.

He snapped on the lamp on the nightstand and squinted at the sudden brightness. Moments later he was once again in darkness, waiting for Rick's wonder drug to provide a reprieve from the throbbing pain.

Tomorrow, he thought, he'd call the nursery to see what arrangements could be made for someone to come over from California to get him and his vehicle. Neither of his brothers or his sister had been at their respective homes when he'd telephoned earlier that evening. And he had not left any message on their answering machines.

There was no doubt in his mind that he did *not* want to leave Memory Lawson. And, just to complicate matters more, he didn't want to leave Honey Heather either.

Drowsiness began to creep over him like a slowly moving fog. He smiled crookedly as the image of a laughing Heather and Memory formed in his mind's eye.

Drew awoke the next morning to bright sunlight filling the room, the tantalizing aroma of coffee wafting through the air, and a dull but bearable ache in his arm.

He showered, covering the cast with the plastic bag Memory had given him the previous night. Though relieved that the painkiller-induced fuzziness of his mind dissipated under the stinging hot water, he decided not to attempt to shave with his left hand. The mere thought of it caused him to cringe as he envisioned accidentally slitting his throat.

He'd just have to look like a bum, he reasoned, running a hand over the rough stubble on his face. It was better to be a breathing bum than a spit-shined dead body.

He returned to the bedroom and, seeing his duffel bag on the floor, was grateful that it had been retrieved from his vehicle. Getting dressed was difficult, but he was relieved to once again be wearing his own clothes, clothes that actually fit.

In the kitchen a cheerful Tina fixed him a huge breakfast, which Drew consumed down to the last bite. He eyed the telephone on the wall, knew he should call Phil and Clark at the nursery in Santa Barbara, then told himself he'd certainly do that . . . later.

"Memory and Heather are with the horses," Tina said as she picked up Drew's empty plate. "Just wander down toward the barn. They're probably by one of the corrals, but you won't have any trouble finding them." She leaned slightly toward him. "You *do* want to see Memory this morning, don't you?"

Drew frowned at the unexpected question. "Well, sure, I want to see her."

"Good, good," Tina said, beaming. "And Heather?"

"Honey Heather?" He smiled. "She's a great kid, isn't she?"

"Oh, yes, a wonderful child. Is your sling snug? Yes, it looks fine. You hurry on down to the corrals. Shoo. You just said you were eager to see Memory and Heather."

"Tina," Drew said, narrowing his eyes, "you wouldn't be trying to matchmake, would you?"

Tina splayed one hand on her ample bosom. "Me?"

"You."

"Well . . ."

He chuckled and got to his feet. "You're obviously deciding whether or not your conscience can handle a little white lie. So I'll make it easy for you. If you *are* trying to matchmake . . ." He paused.

"Yes?"

"Go for it, sweetheart. I can use all the help I can get."

Tina clapped her hands together. "I knew it, I knew it. I could feel it in the air, this marvelous thing that is taking place between you and Memory. But, Drew, you do have a tremendously difficult battle ahead of you."

"I realize that. Memory has built strong walls around herself. Listen, Tina, don't misunderstand me. I'm not saying I'm in love with Memory. All I know is, there's something happening here that might be important. What I want is a chance to find out."

"That's enough, for now, to warm my heart. Go to the corrals."

"I'm gone," he said, heading for the door. "Thanks for the delicious breakfast."

"You're welcome," she called after him. "And thank you," she added to herself, "for coming into my Memory's life. Don't give up on her, Drew Sloan."

Outside, Drew stopped for a moment to fill his lungs with the clean, rain-washed air. He savored new and pleasant scents—the sweet aroma of hay, the heady smell of horses, a light floral fragrance that hinted of wildflowers beginning to bloom.

The aromas of a ranch, he mused. They were pleasant, earthy. There was an aura of peacefulness too, that wasn't present in the hubbub of Santa Barbara. The sounds in the distance of birds singing and horses whinnying were gifts from nature, intertwined with occasional muted voices of men.

Lord, this was a beautiful place, he thought. The ranch had a feeling of order, of everything being in its proper spot and functioning as it should. What an incredible sense of pride Memory must have as she moved through her days on this land.

She hadn't started the ranch from scratch, he knew. It had obviously belonged to her parents, and she'd inherited it at their deaths. Memory Mountain had perhaps gotten its name to celebrate the birth of Memory twenty-six years before.

Looking around, Drew frowned. Why had Memory left her home for heaven only knew where? What had happened to her that she returned years later with a newborn daughter, no husband, and a chip on her shoulder about men?

Memory Lawson was a very complicated woman, he thought as he started walking toward the corrals. She was strong, assertive, didn't take guff from anyone. She was also a loving mother and, from what he'd seen, a good employer. Yet she had a blind spot when it came to men. Her statement the day before that he would have denied any responsibility of fault if Gladstone had canceled bringing in his mare was only one example of her attitude.

She'd made her accusation as though it were a given that men didn't accept responsibility for their actions, that they denied being in the wrong if things went bad.

Well, that wasn't the case when dealing with Drew Sloan, and he'd prove that to her.

He continued walking, though at a slow pace to avoid jarring his arm, enjoying the beautiful morning and the bustling activity of the ranch. He'd almost reached the corral where he thought he'd seen Memory as he'd left the house, when he stopped.

Something was niggling at the back of his mind. He concentrated, mentally pushing away the shadows so he could clearly see what was nagging at him.

Yes, there it was. Just before he'd fallen into his drug-induced sleep the night before, a disturbing question had beat against his brain. Was Memory Lawson lonely?

He started walking again, quickening his step.

There were so many layers to Memory, such incredible depths. He wanted to uncover, discover, and understand all that made up that very intriguing woman.

And never far from the front of his mind, he admitted, smiling, was his burning desire to gather her close and kiss her once again.

Memory was by the corral closest to the barn. She stood staring at the horse within the enclosure, her arms on the top rail, her chin resting on stacked fists.

"Good morning," he said.

She jerked in surprise, then straightened away from the fence and looked at him. "Oh, good morning. Did you sleep well?"

"Yes, after I gave in and took one of Rick's painkillers." He paused as he stared at her. She was so beautiful, with the morning sun pouring over her, gleaming on her dark hair, which was pulled back into a braid. Her clothes were ordinary, a cotton shirt and denim jacket, faded jeans and worn cowboy boots, yet she couldn't have been lovelier if she were dressed in a silk gown with diamonds glittering at her throat and ears. He was going to kiss her. He had to kiss her, right now, in front of her ranch hands and the horses and— *Sloan, get a grip.* He cleared his throat. "He's a nice guy, that Rick."

"Oh? You two didn't seem to hit it off too well at first."

"We . . . well, let's just say we reached an understanding." Drew ran his hand over his chin. "Excuse my appearance. I wasn't brave enough to attempt shaving with my left hand. You certainly were deep in thought when I came up. Is there something wrong with that horse?" He nodded to the one horse in the corral. "It looks like it would do well to go on a diet, but I know zip about horses."

Memory frowned and redirected her attention to the horse. "That's Sugar Shoes, my finest breeding mare. She's from a long line of champions. She's not fat from overeating, she's due to drop a foal in about six to eight weeks. That's extremely valuable cargo she's carrying there."

"Oh, I see," Drew said, nodding.

"Sugar is behaving the way she usually does in the very first stages of her labor. She's restless, jumpy, off her feed. I'm hoping this is a false alarm. It's too early for her to deliver a sound, healthy foal."

"I can understand why you're concerned. You should have seen my family the night my brother Phil's wife, Julie, had my nephew, Trey. Talk about a bunch of shook-up people in the waiting room at the hospital. It's a wonder they didn't toss us all out. Trey was a bit early, but he's fit as a fiddle now. Great kid."

Memory glanced at him. "All of you went to the hospital together?"

"Well, sure. I mean, it was a momentous event, and ol' Phil needed our support. He was a basket case, so we . . ." Drew dropped speaking and shook his head. "Oh, hell, Memory, I'm sorry. You were alone when you had Heather, right?"

She turned to look at Sugar Shoes again, lifting her chin.

"It's not important," she said.

Drew moved closer and stroked her cheek with his thumb, back and forth in a slow rhythm. A tingling sensation danced along Memory's spine, then changed to a thrumming heat deep within her. She took a step sideways, forcing him to drop his hand, and kept her gaze riveted on Sugar.

"It *is* important, Memory," he said, his voice low. "I hate the thought that you were alone when you had Heather. It shouldn't have been like that. I wish—"

"Leave it be, Drew." She turned her head to meet his gaze. "It was more than five years ago and not worth discussing now." It was still too painful to discuss, dammit. She'd never forget how alone she'd felt that long night, how frightened. "Speaking of your brothers, did you call them this morning to make some arrangements for your return to Santa Barbara?"

Drew looked at her for a long moment. "No, I didn't phone. I'll go back up to the house right now and—"

"Drew! Drew! Drew!" a voice called.

He turned to see Heather, two corrals away, perched on the back of a pony. A cowboy was with her, holding a lead rope in one hand and guiding the pony around the edge of the enclosure.

"Look at me, Drew," Heather yelled. "I'm riding my great big horse."

"You sure are, Honey Heather," he hollered back. "You're awesome."

Memory watched him as he watched her daughter, his smile broadening into a wide grin. He might be smiling now, but she'd seen the hurt in his eyes when she'd snapped at him about contacting his family. She'd sounded so cold, making it clear that she wanted him off her ranch as quickly as possible.

She'd felt emotionally cornered again, though. When he'd spoken of his nephew's birth, it had flung her back in time to the seemingly endless nightmare hours preceding Heather's birth. As he'd talked, she'd struggled against the horrendous images swirling around her, trying to escape like a person frantically clawing toward the surface from the depths of a dark, frightening hole of suffocating water.

When she'd mentally managed to escape, Drew had slam-dunked her again into another emotional quandary. He'd been sympathetic, voicing concern over her having been alone that night five years ago.

She'd been going down for the third time, emotionally drained, so she'd struck out in anger, attempting to replace the bricks in her wall that he'd knocked down once more.

Drew was going to leave. He'd been dragging his feet about it, but she'd pushed him into action by verbally attacking him. So he was going to leave.

And the sooner the better, Memory told herself. She didn't want him there, upsetting her emotional applecart at every turn. She didn't want him there, causing her to have sensual dreams through the night of becoming his lover. She didn't want him there, creating visions in her mind of herself, Drew, and Heather, laughing, sharing, having dinner, as a family, a loving unit.

Darn it, she fumed, he had to go away and never return. She could, and would, repair the damage he'd done to her once-solid wall. She'd resume her life as it had been, soon forgetting that Drew Sloan even existed. She'd be Memory Lawson, mother, rancher, horse breeder, alone and lonely in her small, quiet corner of the world.

Her hands tightened on the top rail of the corral fence with such force, her knuckles turned white. Her eyes widened in horror as she stared unseeing at Sugar Shoes, her own thoughts beating unmercifully against her confused mind.

Alone and lonely . . . Alone and lonely . . . lonely . . . lonely . . . lonely . . .

"Memory?"

She jerked her head around to look at Drew. A frown creased his brow as he studied her, the horse, then her again.

"Take it easy," he said gently. "You don't know for certain that Sugar Shoes is in trouble. Maybe she's just . . . Forget it. I don't know anything about horses. Don't worry, though. It tears me up to see . . . Damn."

Frustration at his lack of knowledge of horses and the overpowering need to kiss Memory won the battle within Drew against common sense and self-control. He took one step toward her, closing the distance between them, slid his free arm across her shoulders, dipped his head, and covered her mouth with his.

He drank in the taste of her, savoring, remembering. The softness of her lips sparked heated passion within him, heavy and low in his aching body, and he mentally cursed the bulky cast that kept him from nestling her to him. He burned with desire for her. She was Memory, and this kiss, like the one they'd shared on Memory Mountain, had been worth waiting a lifetime for.

Despite the mist of arousal engulfing him, he realized Memory was returning his ardor in kind, giving as she took, and he inwardly rejoiced. This was it, the turning point of his life. This was the woman he'd searched for. This was what it had all been about.

And this was, possibly, forever.

He parted her lips, those enticing lips, and delved his tongue between them to meet her tongue.

Memory was lost in a swirling sea of desire, the heat of it chasing away a chill she hadn't even known was inside her. It had been with her for so long, she'd accepted it as a natural part of her.

But now, just as when Drew had kissed her before, a warmth filled her, steadily growing. Now there was the wondrous feel of Drew's lips on hers, of his tongue meshing with hers. Now there was the power of his strong arm holding her with a possessiveness that was comforting and right. Now there was the tantalizing aroma of Drew, of soap, sweat, and man.

And, oh, dear heaven, how she wanted him.

"Mommy's kissing Drew!" Heather yelled, suddenly. "I'm going to have a real daddy. Drew's going to be my daddy. Hip hip 'ray!"

Memory's eyes flew open, and she wrenched

herself away from Drew. Her heart racing, she stared at him in horror as harsh reality returned.

"Dear God," she whispered, her voice sounding strange and hoarse, "what have I done? What was I doing?"

"Kissing me," Drew said. He shook his head as if to clear it, then a wide smile broke across his face. "You were kissing me, Miss Memory Mountain, and I must say you were doing a helluva fine job of it."

"Shut up," she hissed. "Don't you dare say another word."

"Mommy!" Heather hollered. "Can I call Betsy and tell her I'm gonna have a daddy now just like her? Can I, Mommy?"

"Oh, good night," Memory said, pressing a hand to her flushed forehead.

Drew leaned toward her, his smile still firmly in place.

"Well, Mommy?" he asked. "Can Heather call Betsy now with the big news?"

"Shut up," she said again, glaring at him. She looked past him to the corral where Heather was still on her pony. "Jesse," she said, amazed that her voice had enough strength to carry that far. "Would you set Heather down, please? Heather, come over here, sweetheart."

A minute later the little girl ran toward them, pigtails flying, eyes sparkling, a smile on her face. She was wearing pink corduroy overalls and a pale pink cotton shirt. Perky pink bows adorned the ends of her braids.

"Hi, Honey Heather," Drew said. "How's life?"

"Heather," Memory said. She hunkered down and took the child's hand in hers. "Listen to me. Drew is *not* going to be your daddy."

Heather's smile faded. "How come?"

"Yeah," Drew said, "how come?"

Memory shot him a murderous look, then redirected her attention to her daughter.

"Betsy said that when people kiss and stuff," Heather said sternly, "it's 'cause they love each other, and when her mommy kissed Jimmy, he got to be her daddy."

"No, Heather, that's not always—"

"Betsy said so," Heather said, her voice rising. "And Jimmy *is* her daddy now. Betsy told me to watch, 'cause if you kissed somebody, then I'd get a daddy too. And I want one." Her lower lip began to tremble. "I want a daddy, Mommy, I do. I do, really. And you kissed Drew, so he's going to be my daddy, no matter what." She sniffled and tears filled her eyes. "That's how it works."

"Sweetie," Memory said, "you don't understand. Betsy is confused about—"

"No, no, no," Heather said, yanking her hands free. "Betsy knows, and she told me, and she got Jimmy for a daddy."

"I— I didn't realize you wanted a daddy," Memory said. "You've never said anything about it."

"Well, I do," the little girl said, tears spilling onto

her cheeks. "And I can have one 'cause you kissed Drew. You can't break the rules. You always tell me not to break the rules. If you don't let Drew be my daddy, then I'll . . . then I'll just hate you, hate you, hate you!" She spun around and ran toward the house.

"Dear God," Memory whispered. She slowly straightened, her fingertips pressed to her lips as she stared after Heather.

"Dammit," Drew said, shaking his head. "Memory, what can I say? I wanted to kiss you so damn much, and I didn't think past that. I'm sorry— No, I'm not sorry that I kissed you, because it was sensational. But I do apologize for upsetting Heather. Hell, what a mess."

Memory sighed. "I'd like nothing better than to blame it all on you, scream and holler at you, but I can't. I responded to your kiss, Drew. I was, stupidly, a willing and cooperative partner in that fiasco."

"There wasn't anything stupid about it."

"Oh, really? Have you already erased the scene with Heather from your tiny mind? That child"— she pointed toward the house—"believes that it is now etched in stone that you're going to be her daddy. And I'm going to be the Wicked Witch of the West if I don't agree to that asinine program."

Drew grinned. "So marry me."

"That does it," Memory said, throwing up her hands. She started toward the house.

"Hey." Drew strode after her, gripping her arm

to halt her. She stopped and glowered at him. "I was just trying to lighten things a bit. Look, I realize this isn't funny. Well, it is sort of cute. You know what I mean? Kids have fascinating minds."

Memory tapped one foot impatiently.

"Yes, well . . . um . . . What are you going to say to Heather? She's really upset. She's not about to buy the fact that people go around kissing other people all the time." He shook his head. "Wrong, Sloan, that sounded gross. How about saying that we're thinking it over, the my-being-her-daddy thing?"

"Don't be absurd."

He wasn't being absurd, Drew thought. That kiss he'd shared with Memory had answered a lot of questions for him. If he wasn't in love with her, he was darn close to it.

"I didn't know," she said quietly, "that Heather wanted a father. How could I have not known that? I thought we were doing fine, the two of us. And she has Franco, plus all the hands who fuss over her. She's never even asked where her father is, why he isn't here with us. I just didn't realize she was so unhappy."

"Don't be so hard on yourself," Drew said. "She's not unhappy. She's a bouncy, smiling little kid. Her friend Betsy got a new daddy, so Heather wants one too. It could have been a bike or a doll. It just happens that some guy named Jimmy married Betsy's mother. If Betsy gets a kitten tomorrow, Jimmy will be old news."

Memory gave him a skeptical look. "Is that so? When did you become such an expert on how a child thinks?"

He shrugged. "I used to be one."

"There are times, Sloan, when you still qualify. You're being terribly naive about this situation with Heather. For her to suddenly start talking about having a father with such intensity makes it very clear that she's been brooding about it for heaven only knows how long."

"Oh." Drew paused. "You're not ripping yourself up because she said she'd hate you, are you? I can remember flinging that one at my dad once, and he didn't even blink. He just said, 'No problem, Drew. I'm not really crazy about you at the moment, either.' That sure took the wind out of my sails. My dad is a great guy."

"So was mine," she said softly. She took a deep breath and let it out slowly. "No, the I hate-you number is normal. No parent likes to hear it, but we do. The important issue is that Heather desperately wants a father, and she now believes I'm the only obstacle standing in the way of your stepping into that role."

The sound of a whinnying horse caused Memory to look back toward the corral.

"Oh, Sugar Shoes, not now. If she's really going into labor . . . Lord, there's just so much to deal with all of a sudden."

"You're not alone, Memory. This problem with

Heather is my fault, and I'll do everything possible to correct the situation."

She kept her gaze on the horse. "I told you that I accept equal responsibility for—for what happened. However, there is something you can do that I feel is the best course of action."

"You name it, you've got it."

She lifted her chin and looked directly into his eyes. "I'd like you to leave the ranch immediately. I'll get a couple of the hands to help. One can take you to Tumbleweed in your vehicle, another can follow to bring the driver back. You can call your family from Rick's, then sleep on the cot at the clinic until someone can come for you."

"But—"

"It's the only way, Drew. I won't be able to convince Heather that Betsy made a mistake while you're still here giving her hope. You've got to leave. Now."

Five

Leave. Now.

Memory's words echoed painfully in Drew's mind as he watched her hurry toward the house. His gaze swept from her to the corral, where Franco was now frowning as he studied Sugar Shoes.

A strange, chilling sense of isolation dropped over Drew as he stared down at the ground. It was as though Memory had drawn a circle in the dust, a boundary within which he had to stay. It was a shadowy sphere, cold, and dark, and lonely.

Leave. Now.

He had kissed Memory Lawson, and, oh, Lord, those kisses had been fantastic. His passion had soared instantly, his desire for Memory so intense, it had shaken him to the very core of his being.

Other emotions had intertwined with the desire

as well. He was inching closer to falling in love with Memory. Might already be in love with her, for all he knew.

Leave. Now.

Dammit, he didn't want to leave, just pack it up and fade into the sunset. Memory was *here*, Heather was *here*, and this was where *he* should be.

To do what? he asked himself. Cause more upset? He'd been trouble with a capital *T* since he'd fallen over his backpack, thoroughly disrupting Memory's life. Now he'd upset Heather, too, caused the little girl to cry as she revealed her secret yearning to have a daddy.

It was understandable, he decided, that Memory wanted him off her ranch. He'd been a royal pain in the tush ever since she'd discovered him trespassing on her private mountain.

Drew sighed, then started back toward the house. There was no point in joining Franco. All Drew knew about horses was that John Wayne rode them in the movies.

And his great spiel about Heather wanting a father today and a kitten tomorrow had been a crock. He didn't know squat about little kids' psyches either.

The nursery business, he knew. Existing in the wilds, hiking, camping, fishing, he knew. But at the moment there wasn't a long line of people forming who wanted to tap into his two areas of expertise. He was so useless on the ranch, it was a sin. He'd caused nothing but grief since he'd arrived.

And so he'd leave.

For now.

Drew quickened his step. Yes, he'd go, but there was one fact that could be taken all the way to the bank. He would be back.

Memory sat on the edge of Heather's canopy bed, holding the little girl on her lap.

"And that's exactly how my mother explained it to me," she said, "when I was just about the same age you are now. It's fine to cry, Heather, when you're unhappy, but remember that the angels are waiting."

"But, Mommy, can't the angels wait some more? I have to cry 'cause you won't let Drew be my daddy."

"The angels will wait," Memory said. "But that's not going to change anything. Betsy made a mistake, and you have to accept that. Crying isn't going to make things different."

Heather sighed. "Well, then I guess I won't cry anymore, not if the angels are waiting to sing and stuff."

"That's right. Angels singing, angels sad."

"Angels singing," Drew repeated quietly.

Memory and Heather both looked over to the doorway, where Drew was standing with one shoulder propped against the frame.

"How long have you been there?" Memory asked. "I didn't hear you come down the hall."

"Tina told me where you were. I heard the whole story about the angels. It's a really nice one."

"I'm going to stop crying now, Drew," Heather said, "so the angels will sing, but I wish you were going to be my daddy. I really, really do."

Drew was silent as he gazed at the two of them. Beautiful, he thought. He'd remember forever the picture of the two of them on Heather's bed, with their matching dark hair and eyes, delicate features, velvety soft skin. And if Heather still wished he was going to be her daddy, well, he wished for the same thing.

Because . . .

He straightened.

Because he was in love with Memory Lawson.

It was so clear that it seemed impossible that he'd been a muddled mess just a short time ago, confused about his feelings for Memory.

"Drew?" Memory said. "Is something wrong? You have the strangest look on your face."

"What? Oh, no, nothing is wrong, not at all, far from it. Everything is just great. Superb."

"I'm glad to hear it," she said, eyeing him warily.

He smiled. "Honey Heather, the angels are singing. Oh, yes, sweetheart, the angels are definitely singing."

Drew's smile was infectious and Heather matched it, adding a tinkling, little-girl giggle.

"Say," he said, "what's the name of that great big horse you were riding?"

"Ralph," Heather said, sliding off Memory's lap.

"Ralph?" he repeated. "You named your pony Ralph?"

She nodded decisively.

"There was no discussion on the subject," Memory said. "She saw him and said, 'Hi, Ralph.' That was that."

"I love it," Drew said, chuckling.

"Guess what, Drew?" Heather said. "If you were my daddy and lived here, you could have a horse that was all your own."

"Heather," Memory said, a warning tone to her voice as she got to her feet. "That's enough."

"Well, he could."

Memory opened her mouth to reply, then stopped as she saw Tina appear behind Drew in the doorway. Drew stepped aside so that Tina could enter the room.

"Franco called from the barn," Tina said. "Sugar Shoes is definitely in labor. Franco phoned the vet. He's on his way."

"Oh, no," Memory said. "I'll go to the barn right now. Heather, please stay in the house with Tina."

"Come with me, Heather," Tina said as Memory ran from the room. "You can help make chocolate chip cookies."

"Yes, yes," the little girl said, clapping her hands.

The pair left the bedroom, but Drew remained there, frowning.

"Hello, Sloan," he said aloud. "How's it going, buddy? Feeling useless? Hell, yes."

He sighed, shook his head, and walked slowly from the room.

Darkness had long since fallen, but Memory remained in the double-wide stall where Sugar Shoes lay sleeping. She sat in the fresh straw, her back against the wooden wall, arms wrapped around drawn-up knees.

No one else was in the barn, and except for an occasional whinny or snort from one of the other horses, all was silent.

She was exhausted, and she'd lost all track of time. She should go to the house, but it seemed too great an effort. She didn't want to move or even think.

"Memory?"

She turned her head. Drew stood at the edge of the stall.

"Franco told us that the foal died," he said quietly. "I'm sorry. I really am."

She nodded.

"He said that Sugar Shoes would be all right. That's good news."

She nodded again, but still didn't speak.

"Memory, it's been over two hours since Franco came up to the house. Tina put Heather to bed, and I read her a story. I couldn't handle it any longer, waiting for you, wondering if you were okay. I stayed in the house because I knew I'd just be in the way down here, but now . . . Memory, come on up to the house. There's nothing more for you to do here."

"No," she said, her voice sounding as weary as she felt. "I just want to sit here a while longer."

"Why?"

"I . . . I don't know."

"Well, if that's what you want to do, then that's what we'll do."

He eased himself to the floor next to her, resting his back against the wall, their shoulders lightly touching. He stretched his long legs out in front of him and crossed them at the ankle.

"You don't have to stay," she said, staring at her knees.

He shrugged. "You don't either." He glanced around. "This is a big stall."

"It's the birthing stall."

"Oh. Sugar Shoes is sure zonked. Do horses snore?"

A small smile flitted across Memory's lips.

"You're pretty upset about the foal, huh?" he said gently.

"It was meant to be. It had a deformed heart, and nature took care of things."

"Oh. Franco didn't go into details. Well, if you're accepting what happened to the baby, and you know Sugar is going to be fine, why are you still sitting here?"

She leaned her head back and closed her eyes.

"I don't know, Drew. I just suddenly didn't have the energy to move an inch. I knew Heather was being tended to, and I gave in to whatever strange mood this is. It's peaceful here, quiet, almost like another world. The financial setback from losing the foal will create some budgeting problems, but I've worked through things like that before. Sugar is weak, but she'll bounce back. I honestly don't know why I'm still out here."

"You don't really have to know, I guess. Do you mind if I stay with you for a bit?"

"If you want to, it's fine with me, but it's not very comfortable."

"That's all right. I need to do research on whether or not horses snore."

Memory didn't answer, and he looked at her. She was exhausted, he thought. He could see the purple smudges beneath her eyes, and the unnatural pallor of her skin. She should be sound asleep in her bed.

After several minutes she opened her eyes again, but didn't look at him. "Sugar's foal was beautiful," she said. "It was perfectly formed, so tiny. There was no evidence of its heart problem. It was such a pretty foal, and it was hard to believe that it was dead after only being here a few minutes."

"It's really too bad, Memory."

"Yes, well. I understand that these things happen." She drew in a deep, shuddering breath. "It does help when you can understand the 'why' of death and say good-bye. When—when my parents were killed in a small-plane crash, no one could tell me why it had been them, such wonderful people, such warm, loving parents, and . . ." Her voice trailed off.

Drew waited, hardly breathing, his heart racing so fast, it actually hurt. Memory was baring her soul to him, talking about the death of her parents. She was giving him at that moment, in that quiet barn, a precious gift that he would cherish. The woman he loved was sharing with him feelings she'd buried deep inside of her.

"Go on, Memory," he prompted.

"They were dead," she said, her tear-filled eyes meeting his. "The plane . . . exploded on impact and . . . There was a memorial service but no burial because there was . . . nothing left . . . nothing left to send home."

"Ah, Memory."

He slid his arm around her shoulders and eased her closer. She complied, resting her head on his chest, being careful not to bump his cast.

"I didn't understand," she said, nearly choking on a sob, "and I didn't know how to say good-bye."

He kissed the top of her head, but didn't speak, aware that he'd never get words past the lump in his throat. He really didn't know, either, what to say.

Several minutes passed in silence.

"How strange," Memory said finally, not moving. "I don't like to talk about my parents' death. I have no idea why I said all that to you."

"Because I was listening. Because like it or not, there's a part of you that knows I care deeply for you, and that you feel at least something for me. Because you're aware that you can trust me."

She started to pull away, but he tightened his hold.

"Memory, don't. Don't run. Don't go back behind your walls. I'm not going to hurt you." He loved her, but if he told her that now, she'd bolt like a frightened fawn. "You have nothing to fear from me."

Yes, she did! Memory cried silently. Drew Sloan was dangerous. He was having a tremendous impact on her, both physically and emotionally. Her control was steadily slipping away, like sand that could not be stopped from sifting through fingers intent on holding it fast.

The kisses she had shared with Drew had left her shaken to the core, and aching for more. The part of her that was woman wanted him, desired him with a near-shattering intensity. The mere thought of meshing her body with his, becoming one, caused heat to swirl deep within her.

The part of her that was mother smiled warmly when she watched Drew interact with Heather. Her daughter had revealed a heartfelt yearning to have a father, to claim Drew as her daddy, and Memory felt sure he'd be a picture-perfect one.

The part of Memory Lawson that was horse breeder extraordinaire now wished for a partner to share in the triumphs, and to lean on during the defeats such as the one that had taken place that night as Sugar Shoes' foal had fought and lost its battle for life.

Nothing to fear from Drew Sloan? The very structure of her existence was at risk. She could not, would not, go one step farther along the path to destruction.

No!

Memory jerked free of Drew's hold and got to her feet, moving quickly out of the stall. Drew followed her, grasping her arm to halt her flight before she could go farther.

"I'm going to the house," she said, looking at the top button on his shirt. "I'm very tired and—"

"You're running, Memory. You're running from me *and* yourself."

She looked up at him, eyes narrowed in anger. "I am *not* running, Drew Sloan, I'm . . ." She stopped. "All right, I *am* running. I won't deny that, because it's true. Yes, you turn me on. Is that what you want to hear? Does that give your ego a rush? So you're capable of pushing my sexual buttons. Big macho deal. Hey, Drew, we're in a barn. We could have an authentic roll in the hay. Does that trip your trigger?"

He clenched his teeth, a muscle jerking in his jaw as his own anger rose. "Knock it off, dammit. There's nothing cheap or sordid about what's happening between us. You can run all the way to Toledo, but you won't escape from the facts. This is real and honest between us. It's good, Memory."

"It's nothing, Drew."

"The hell it isn't."

He moved his hand from her arm to the nape of her neck and lowered his head, claiming her mouth in a hard, searing kiss that spoke of anger, frustration, and unquelled passion. In the next instant, though, a groan rumbled from his chest and the kiss gentled.

Memory was consumed by an amalgam of sensual sensations, one tumbling into the next, heightening her desire. She gripped Drew's shoulders and moved as close to him as his cast would allow. Her tongue met his, stroking in a rhythm that matched the pulsing deep within her. In total abandon, she answered the demands of his mouth, and her smoldering passion burst into a raging flame.

Drew slipped his right arm free of the sling as his other arm encircled Memory's back. He nestled her to him, the ecstasy of at last feeling her feminine softness pressed to his hard body flinging him further out of control.

He kept the cast away from her, only his fingertips resting against her waist in a feathery touch. His arousal was full and heavy, and he ached for the exquisite release he knew Memory could give him.

"I want you," he murmured, his lips against hers. "I've never wanted anyone as much as I do you. That sounds so corny, so false, but it's true."

"I want you, too, Drew. I thought I would never

want any man again, but . . . Oh, yes, I do want to make love with you."

"Not here," he said. "Not in the barn. I couldn't handle it if you had regrets, if you believed in the morning that what we shared was just what you said, a roll in the hay."

"I won't be sorry, I promise you that. This barn will be a private place, our place. We can't go to the house. Tina and Franco live in the wing beyond the kitchen, and Heather is there."

He brushed his lips over hers, then traced the shape of her mouth with the tip of his tongue. She trembled.

"Please," she whispered. "There's no world beyond the two of us, right here, right now." No thoughts, no reality, she added silently. No shadows or ghosts from the past. "Make love with me."

"Yes."

He captured her mouth once more in a long, torrid kiss. Finally she found the strength to move away and lead him down the wide, dimly lit corridor to a small room at the end of the barn.

She flipped the light switch, bringing alive a lamp on an end table next to a single bed. She closed and locked the door, then frowned as she glanced around.

"We have this set up in case we're putting in a vigil with a sick horse. But the bed is so narrow. What about your arm?"

Lord, listen to her, she thought. She was analyzing the situation like a brazen women who slept with anything in pants. Forget it. She didn't care what she sounded like. The night had an other-worldly quality to it. All that mattered was Drew.

"Don't worry about my arm," he said, smiling. "I just have to remember not to thunk you in the head with the cast." He paused, his smile fading. "Memory, are you sure about this? You've promised me that you won't regret it, but are you positive you can keep that promise? This is too important to—"

She placed two fingertips against his lips. "Make love with me, Drew Sloan. Please."

"It will be my pleasure, Memory Lawson."

It was a small barely furnished room in a barn, but it was theirs, and that night it took on an aura of opulent splendor.

The bed was narrow, the sheets freshly washed but frayed from use. The mattress was thin and lumpy. But it was theirs, as welcoming as the biggest bed with expensive satin sheets might be.

The clothes they removed were faded jeans and much-worn shirts. But on this night, they were Cinderella and the Prince, shedding splendid evening clothes after returning from the glamorous, glittering ball.

Drew's cumbersome cast could not be ignored. He had to keep it off Memory's body, and not lean his own weight on the broken arm. That nuisance combined with the narrow bed caused them to start and stop, shift and move. But it was their night, and they were lovers, graceful, knowing, totally in tune, perfectly matched.

"Lord, you're beautiful," Drew said.

"So are you."

He skimmed his lips over the velvet softness of her skin, leaving a heated path in their wake. His tongue flicked across the nipple of one of her breasts, then he took the sweet bounty into his mouth. Memory sighed in pure pleasure.

Her hands roamed over his back, relishing, savoring, the feel of the taut muscles bunching and moving beneath her palms.

They kissed and caressed, each discovering the wondrous mysteries of the other's body. Their breathing became rough and labored, echoing in the small room, and their skin was flushed from passion's rising flame.

They yearned, ached, burned, with the need to become one, giving and taking, seeking and finding the ecstasy they knew awaited them.

But they held back, the anticipation of what was to come sweet torture. Hands and lips seemed ubiquitous, wants grew urgent, kisses were hungry with need.

"Oh, Drew, please," Memory whispered. "Now. Please. Come to me now."

"Yes. I want—Ow!" he exclaimed as the cast struck the wall.

With a boldness that would have shocked her if

she stopped to think about it, Memory took charge. She sat up and, not speaking, urged Drew to lie down on his back. Stretching out on top of him, she kissed him, her tongue plummeting deep within his mouth. A tremor swept through his body, and his left hand clutched her.

Slowly, slowly she inched upward, then raised her hips, straddled his, and took him into the heated haven of her femininity.

"Oh . . . Drew," she whispered.

Drew couldn't speak. He was too overcome by the magnificent beauty of their joining, and the intensity of the love he had for this woman.

He began the rocking tempo, and he groaned. She moved faster, harder, and he met her rhythm in perfect synchronization.

Never, Memory thought hazily, had she experienced anything like this. She was acutely aware of the wondrous differences between woman and man, of the perfect blending of gentle curves and rugged contours. Drew was deep within her, filling her, taking her higher and higher to a place she'd never been.

The tension within her was building, coiling and hot. They moved as one entity with a thundering cadence . . . reaching . . . higher . . . closer . . .

"Drew!"

"Oh, yes, Memory. Yes!"

They reached the summit and were flung into

oblivion, calling each other's names. They hovered there, suspended in time and space, as the last of the exquisite waves rippled through them.

Memory collapsed onto Drew's chest, spent and sated, her face buried in the crook of his neck. He wrapped his free arm around her waist, holding her fast, as though he'd never let her go.

Seconds ticked into minutes. Heartbeats returned to normal, bodies cooled, breathing slowed. Memory stirred, but Drew tightened his hold.

"Don't go," he said softly. "Not yet."

She wiggled down a bit so she could lay her cheek on his chest, then shifted her legs so she was once again stretched along the length of him.

"Oh, my," she said, with a contented sigh.

"Incredible." He lifted up enough to kiss her forehead, then his head dropped back onto the pillow. "Fantastic."

"Yes."

"Memory, I . . ."

I love you, he finished silently. Lord, how he wanted to say those words out loud. He'd whisper them first, for only Memory to hear, then later shout them from the rooftops. He was in love with Memory Lawson. She was his.

But he knew the proper time had still not come to tell her of his love. Even more, Memory was *not* his. She had not said anything that indicated how she felt about him.

Before he thoroughly depressed himself, Drew

decided, he'd focus on the positive. Memory *had* told him about her parents. And most definitely on the positive list was the exquisite, beautiful-beyond-description lovemaking he'd just shared with her.

For someone who expressed in no uncertain terms that she didn't need some dolt of a guy in her life, and who hid behind protective walls to assure her solitude, she had given totally of herself as they'd made love.

Given totally of herself to *him*.

Those counted for something, he reasoned. No, they counted for a lot. Memory Lawson might not be his right now but, by damn, she would be. He had no intention of giving up his quest to win her love.

"I could . . ." she yawned. ". . . fall asleep right here."

"Go for it," he said, smiling. "I can't be any lumpier than this mattress."

"No, I'm going to muster my last ounce of energy and go to the house."

"I guess I'll stay put. It's just too much trouble to move."

She dropped a kiss on his lips, then slipped off the bed and began to dress. He watched her, realizing that for some insane reason, observing Memory putting *on* her clothes was as sexually arousing as seeing her take them *off*.

"Memory," he said, tearing his gaze from her

body to look at her face. "About the promise you made . . ."

"Drew, I don't regret anything that happened in this room tonight."

"Good. Okay. That's good."

She went to the door and unlocked it. "Good night, Drew."

He smiled at her. "Good night, Memory."

She opened the door, then glanced back at him over her shoulder. "Is eight A.M. all right with you?"

"To do what?"

"Be driven to Rick's. That plan was forgotten today because of Sugar Shoes. Heather's determination to have you as a daddy hasn't changed. She only stopped crying about it so that the angels would sing. She's not going to give up on the idea until you're actually gone. Eight o'clock tomorrow morning?"

"Dammit, Memory," he said, lunging up to a sitting position, "what is this? You're still trying to get rid of me after our lovemaking? What about us? What about giving us a chance to see where we might be going together?"

"Drew, I promised you I wouldn't regret this night, and I don't. It was . . . it was wonderful. I've never felt so . . . Well, enough said on the subject. What I did *not* promise you is anything *beyond* this night."

"You're turning this," he yelled, sweeping his

free arm over the bed, "into a tacky one-night stand?"

"Not in *my* mind," she said. "If you choose to label it that, I really don't give a tinker's damn." She marched from the room.

"Lawson," he hollered, "you come back here!"

"Sloan," she called back, "go to hell!"

Six

More than two hours later, Memory sighed, punched her pillow, and mumbled several very unladylike words.

A person, she thought dismally, was not capable of falling asleep when said person was carrying on a heated argument with herself. A battle had been raging in her mind ever since she'd left the barn.

She'd *had* to insist that Drew leave the ranch as quickly as possible. It was imperative, for Heather's emotional well-being and for her own, that Drew vanish from their lives.

But she didn't want him to go. Plus, she felt terrible, simply awful, that their stolen night, the precious time when they'd made such exquisite love, had ended in a screaming match.

Memories of their lovemaking filled her, despite

her efforts to push them aside. The now familiar heat of desire suffused her, pulsing deep within her and raising a warm flush to her cheeks.

She wiggled on the bed, giving her body firm directives to stop it that very instant, to return to being under *her* command, *her* control.

Her body, she realized, was not listening.

"Damn you, Drew," she said aloud.

She sighed again. No, she couldn't blame him for her physical and emotional turmoil. She'd like nothing better than to dump it all on him, naming him the villain as she tossed him off her land. But facts were facts, truths were truths. She had to accept responsibility for her own actions. She had, for reasons she couldn't fathom, told Drew about her parents' death and the lingering sorrow that still possessed a corner of her heart and soul.

And she had wanted to make love with him, her need overpowering and undeniable. The meshing of their bodies, their becoming one, was like nothing she had ever known.

Her word was good, her promise kept. She did not regret what they had shared. She just wished she didn't feel so torn in two, pushed and pulled between wishing Drew would stay and demanding that he go.

She finally dozed, but her slumber was restless, filled with vivid dreams that made no sense. When she left her bed at dawn, her eyes felt gritty from lack of sleep, and a weariness consumed her from head to toe.

She would bid Drew Sloan adieu that morning, she thought as she headed for the shower, and she'd do it calmly and coolly .

Even if it killed her.

"How come, Drew?" Heather asked.

Memory stopped just out of sight of the kitchen doorway as she heard Heather's question. Her daughter sounded upset.

"I have to leave," Drew answered, "because my family is expecting me back so that I can do my share of work at our business. It was my turn for a little vacation, but I have to go home now."

"You can't work," Heather said, "'cause your bone broke."

"Good point. But there are things I can do at a plant nursery even with a broken arm. I can answer the phone, talk to customers and answer their questions, stuff like that."

"You can answer *my* phone."

"Sweetheart," he said gently, "listen, I'd love to stay. Believe me, I would *really* love to stay, but I just can't."

"But then . . . but then . . . ," Heather said, tears evident in her voice, "how are you going to be my daddy if you're not here?"

Memory hurried into the kitchen.

"Good morning," she sang out, plastering a smile onto her face. "How is everyone this beautiful, bright, sunny morning?"

Heather folded her arms across her tiny chest and scowled. Drew frowned.

"My, my," Memory said, forcing lightness into her voice. "What a pair. Grumpy and Grouchy. No smiles today?"

"No," Heather said.

Drew didn't reply, and Memory made certain that she didn't look directly at him as she crossed the room to pour herself some coffee.

Nice try, Memory, Drew thought, narrowing his eyes as he watched her. But he knew her smile was phony, and her chirpy-cheerful voice was a farce. She was so tight and tense, she'd probably snap in two if she made a sudden move.

Interesting, he mused on, rather smugly. Miss Memory Mountain was a walking, talking contradiction of her lousy statement the previous night.

He'd felt as though he'd been sucker-punched when she'd announced in her frosty voice that she hadn't promised anything beyond that one night. Yet if what they had shared had meant nothing more than a one-night stand to her, why was she all shook-up today? She had yet to meet his eyes, and she looked like she hadn't slept well.

He refused to believe her odd behavior stemmed from her now regretting their lovemaking. Instead, he guessed their one night together held more importance to her than she was willing to admit.

He smiled broadly and turned to Heather. "Cheer up," he said. "Things are not all bad."

"Yes, they are," the little girl said sullenly.

Tina entered the kitchen from the mud room, nestling a small wicker basket against her chest. She beamed at the trio.

"The chickens gave us big eggs today," she said, "and here's my family waiting for their breakfast. It will be ready in a jiffy."

Memory's eyes widened in shock at Tina's choice of words, then she shot the housekeeper a stormy glare. Tina totally ignored her as Drew chuckled and Heather continued to pout.

"So, sit, sit," Tina said. "I can't cook with everyone under my feet. Heather, your face is all wrinkled up like a raisin. Memory, you didn't get enough sleep. You look terrible. Drew, that beard is disgusting. You could easily pass for a wandering hobo."

Drew laughed as he sat down at the table. Heather slid onto her chair. Memory hesitated, then joined them, still averting her eyes from Drew.

"I can't shave with my left hand," he said. "I'm into living."

"Well, Franco will shave you," Tina said, cracking an egg into a bowl. "He's moving some horses to the north pasture, but he'll be back in a couple of hours."

"Drew won't be here," Memory said. She concentrated on placing her napkin on her lap with just-so precision.

"No?" Tina glanced over at the table. "Where are you off to, Drew?"

Heather folded her arms on the tabletop, then propped her chin on them.

"Home," she said, and sighed dramatically. "Drew's gotta go home to answer the phone and stuff."

"I see," Tina said, nodding. She began to beat the eggs with a whisk. "Well, I'll miss having you here with us, Drew."

"Me, too," Heather said. "Lots and lots."

"Thank you," Drew said, staring at Memory. She continued to smooth the napkin on her lap. "That's really nice to hear. I haven't been here long, but I feel as though I've known you forever. I hate leaving you." He paused. "*All* of you."

Do *not* look at that man, Memory told herself sternly. Not now. Not when he'd just said "*All* of you" in a voice that had dropped to a low, sensual tone that sent both shivers and heat dancing through her. Do *not* take your eyes off your napkin.

Slowly, as if of their own volition, her eyes shifted upward, colliding with Drew's. Her breath caught as she saw the raw desire in the depths of his eyes, the message of want that she feared was evident in *her* eyes as well.

Her heart beat wildly, and a flush stained her cheeks. Panic gripped her, and she had the urge to jump to her feet and run from the room.

She couldn't move, though.

She was pinned in place, held immobile, by Drew's mesmerizing eyes. The stark hunger she saw there softened, changing to a gentleness that seemed to float over her like a caress, stoking the flame of desire within her to a raging fire.

Her breasts grew heavy, yearning for his soothing touch, the mastery of his hands, the sweet homage of his mouth. She wanted to hear him say her name in a voice rough with passion, see his brown eyes become smoky pools, taste his skin, inhale the aroma that was uniquely him and incredibly male.

And she did not want him to leave.

Oh, saints above, she thought frantically, she wasn't, was she? She couldn't be, could she? She just wouldn't, would she?

No! But . . . was she falling in love with Drew?

"Mommy?"

Memory blinked, then snapped her head around to look at Heather.

"Yes?" she said. Her voice squeaked, and she cleared her throat. "Yes?"

"Can I take Dog to my school today for show-and-tell?"

Drew tuned out Memory's explanation of why Dog couldn't go to school as he mentally directed his body to cool it.

He was dying. He had no idea how long he'd sat there drowning in the dark, dark pools of Memory's eyes. What he *did* know—damn, did he ever know—was that she had just caused the smoldering ember of desire within him to burst into a white-hot fire.

He was burning, aching. His arousal was straining against the zipper of his jeans. He wouldn't leave his chair and the protective cover of the table even if someone yelled that they'd dropped a bomb.

What about Memory? he wondered. She'd slipped into her mother mode, and was blithering on about how Dog wouldn't like the seat belts in the school bus. But a minute earlier she'd been a sensual, aroused woman, a woman who wanted him. He'd seen it, the desire in her eyes, the need that matched his own.

More than that, he knew she had sensed the love he felt for her intertwining with his desire. He knew, because he'd seen the panic that crossed her face and settled in her eyes.

"Breakfast," Tina said, snapping Drew out of his reverie as she set two platters on the table. "Memory, pass out the plates. Heather, you do the silverware. Now then, let's see all the eggs and bacon disappear in a flash. Toast is coming right up."

The trio dug into the steaming food, eating in silence for several minutes.

"Know what, Drew?" Heather said finally.

"No, what?"

"I was borned in California."

"Oh, really?" He slid a glance at Memory. She didn't meet his gaze.

"Yep, I was," Heather said, nodding. "Know what? Mickey Mouse lives in California. I didn't see him when I was borned 'cause I was a teeny, teeny, little baby, but he still lives there. My mommy said that someday we can go there, to where Mickey Mouse is."

"That sounds great," Drew said. "I live in California, you know."

"Did you ever see Mickey Mouse?"

"As a matter of fact, I did. He hangs out at a place called Disneyland, and I went there."

Heather dropped her fork onto her plate and scrambled to her knees on her chair.

"You saw Mickey Mouse?" she asked, her hands pressed to her cheeks, eyes wide as saucers. "Honest? You really, really saw Mickey Mouse?"

"Really, really. And Minnie Mouse too. Snow White was there, bopping around with the Seven Dwarfs, and—"

"Heather," Memory interrupted, "your eggs are getting cold. Sit back down in your chair."

Heather ignored her mother and leaned forward, her big dark eyes dancing with excitement.

"Mommy, Drew saw Mickey Mouse."

"Yes, I heard, sweetheart. Finish your breakfast, please."

"When can we go to California?" Heather asked, not moving. "When, Mommy? I want to go to Dizzyland."

"Mickey lives in Disneyland," Drew said pleasantly. "Dis . . . ney . . . land. Great place, Disneyland. Just loads of fun."

Memory glared at him, then redirected her attention to her daughter. "We'll discuss this later, Heather."

"I want to 'cuss it now."

Drew chuckled. Memory glowered at him again.

"Heather," she said, "I don't want to have to get cross with you. I'm not saying this again. Sit back down and finish your breakfast."

Heather executed one of her dramatic sighs and plopped down on the chair. Picking up the fork, she jammed it into the pile of fluffy eggs on her plate.

"Into the mouth," Memory said firmly.

Heather shoveled in some eggs, managing to maintain her pouty expression.

"Your face is going to freeze like that, Honey Heather," Drew said.

She giggled and smiled at him.

"Ah," he said, "there's my pretty girl. I'd know that smile anywhere."

My pretty girl? Memory's mind echoed. Oh, darn, that had sounded so lovely. Heather was Drew's pretty girl, and Memory was Drew's . . .

She frowned and took a bite of toast that she really didn't taste.

Just what exactly, she wondered, was she to Drew? He'd said that he cared for her, had become angry when she'd announced that their lovemaking had been glorious, but that it was only a one-time experience, not a promise for the future.

What did they all mean, the things that Drew said and did? And why on earth should she believe for a single second that any of it was real, honest, and sincere? Even more, why was she wasting her depleted mental energies dwelling on any of this?

Because, she admitted wearily, she had now asked herself a question that couldn't be ignored. Was she falling in love with Drew Sloan?

Forget it. The question could and would be ignored, as well as the emotions churning within her that had prompted her to ask it in the first place. And that, thank you very much, was that.

She drained the last of her coffee and stood. After carrying her dishes to the sink, she turned to Drew.

"I'll go down to the barn," she said, "and see who's free to take you into Tumbleweed."

"I'll walk with you," he said, pushing back his chair and rising.

"No, I—"

"Leave those dishes, Drew," Tina interrupted. "I'd rather tote them than see you do a juggling act with the china."

He chuckled, then looked at Heather. "I'm going to collect a big hug from you before I leave, Honey Heather."

"Well," she said, "I don't want you to go." She shrugged. "So I gotta cry some more."

"And make the angels sad?" he asked. "No, we'll smile and laugh, because singing angels are much nicer. Okay?"

"No."

"You're as stubborn as your mama," he said, patting the girl on the head.

"I'll be back in a bit, Heather," Memory said, starting toward the rear door. "Be a member of the Clean Plate Club today."

Outside, Drew filled his lungs with the crisp morning air.

"I really like the way it smells here," he said as they walked toward the barn. "The aromas are all mixed up together, and it's nature personified."

Memory nodded but didn't speak.

"So," he said, "Heather was born in California."

"Yes."

"I'm no expert on the workings of a little girl's mind, but don't you think it's strange that she's never asked about her father?"

Memory didn't reply, and he slid a glance at her, the tempo of his heartbeat increasing as he waited to see what she would say. He was treading on dangerous ground, he knew, edging toward a subject that was strictly taboo.

Still, Memory *had* told him about her parents' death. So why not press about the faceless, un-named man who had caused her to build the walls around herself?

"I—I've been kidding myself," she finally said. "I had convinced myself that since Heather hadn't asked about her father, it meant she felt no need to know, was doing fine with the father figures here on the ranch."

"You could be right."

"No. She's obviously dwelled on it and talked it over with Betsy. Maybe they decided that Heather shouldn't ask me about her father because it would make me sad. Betsy's father was killed in a hunting accident about a year and a half ago, and I can remember Betsy saying that her mother cried whenever Betsy talked about him."

"So Heather didn't ask you about *her* father. That makes sense."

"I accepted it at face value," Memory went on, "because it was easier. I knew I'd have to answer Heather's questions at some point, but I was willing to postpone it."

"Why? I mean, this *is* the nineties, Memory. You, as a woman, have choices. You decided not to marry Heather's father, so—"

"I didn't decide anything of the kind." She stopped walking, causing him to do the same. "I was a fool, a gullible fool. How do I tell my daughter that? I had suddenly rebelled against my life here and wanted some excitement, adventures, a taste of the world beyond this ranch."

"That's understandable."

"In principle, but I went about it all wrong." She stared across the corrals, where horses grazed. "I was reckless, and I lost touch with who I really was. I went to Los Angeles, got a job as a receptionist in a large advertising agency, bought fancy clothes and enough cosmetics to open a store. I was moving in the fast lane before I realized it, swept up in a crowd that was out for nothing more than a good time."

"Still understandable."

She shook her head fiercely. "It was disgusting. I became involved with a man named Jack who . . . I was in love with him, and convinced myself that he loved me. Oh, Lord, what a joke." She drew in a deep breath to keep her voice steady. "I was an ornament, a pretty toy to him, something to be displayed. Whenever I tried to talk to him about my thoughts and feelings, he'd change the subject, just wouldn't listen. Even the smallest thing that hinted at being upsetting, such as my having a bad day at work, was taboo."

"Memory . . ." Drew lifted his hand, hesitated, then dropped it back to his side.

"I followed his rules," she went on, still not looking at Drew, "believing that was how it was between a man and a woman. I didn't have the experience, the ability, to tell fact from fiction, truth from lies. I doubt that I ever will in regard to men."

"Memory, that's not fair. You've built walls around yourself because of what one man did?"

She whirled to face him. "Because of what *I* did. I fell prey to a smooth line and phony promises. Who's to say I wouldn't be a victim again? No, thank you. I really don't care to run that risk."

"That's crazy," he said, dragging his hand through his hair. "You're older now and—"

"Wiser? I doubt it. Oh, I learned not to trust my judgment in regard to men. If that makes me wiser, then yes, I am."

"Lord, Memory, he was only one man out of millions."

"He was Heather's father," she said, her voice rising, "the man I'd chosen to be my first lover. When I told him I was pregnant, he wrote me a check and said that I should take care of the problem. Our baby was a 'problem.' I refused and he said our relationship was over. He laughed at me, Drew, and told me to go back to my farm. But if I ever grew up and learned the rules of the real world, he'd be glad to see me again."

Drew muttered an earthy expletive.

"I went to San Francisco," she continued, her voice flat. "I used the months waiting for Heather to be born to straighten out my head, reaffirm who I was and where I belonged, and then I brought my baby home."

"And sentenced yourself to a lonely life."

"My life is just fine the way it is."

"Really? Am I to assume from what you're saying that what we shared last night was no big deal? It was just something to do at the moment, because, after all, your life is perfect? You don't need me or anyone. Am I getting this straight, Memory? Was our lovemaking actually casual sex?"

"No!" She planted her fists on her hips. "Damn you, Drew Sloan, don't you dare cheapen what happened. I'll cherish the memories of our night. It *was* making love. It was beautiful and precious, and meant more to me than I can ever begin . . ." She stopped speaking, her eyes wide with horror as she realized what she'd said. ". . . to tell you," she finished in a small voice.

"Good." He dropped a quick kiss on her lips. "Very good, because that's how I feel about it too."

"Now wait a minute."

"We'd better get this show on the road. Heather is still hung up on wanting me to be her daddy. She'll forget that plan once I'm no longer here. My absence will give you the space you'll need to talk to her, explain that picking a daddy for her is *your* job, not hers. You ought to have her all squared away by the time I . . . Well, let's go."

He started toward the barn again, his long legs quickly covering the ground. Memory scrambled after him, halting him by grabbing the back of his shirt.

"Stop right there, Sloan."

He did as instructed, then looked at her with an expression of pure innocence.

"Yes, Lawson?"

"I'll have Heather all squared away by the time you do what? Finish that sentence."

"Oh. Well, surely you know what I was going to say."

"Finish . . . the . . . sentence," she said through clenched teeth.

"By the time, my lovely Miss Memory Mountain, I come back."

Seven

Drew turned the page in the book, jotted down a note to himself, and continued reading.

"Hello, hello," a woman sang out.

"Hi," Drew said, his gaze remaining riveted on the page in front of him.

"Drew Sloan, you've become a dud. Ever since you got back from your jaunt to Arizona, you've been a bookworm, a social dropout, a—"

"Go for it, Mercy," he said, still not looking at his sister. "You're on a roll."

Mercy Sloan Murretti clicked her tongue in exasperation, then leaned across Drew's desk and flattened both hands on the book.

"Hey!" His head snapped up, and he glared at his sister.

She glared right back. Mercy was the baby of the

family, but could hold her own against her three big brothers, Clark, Drew, and Phil.

Clark and Mercy had inherited their mother's auburn hair, while Phil and Drew had brown hair like their father. All four of the Sloan offspring, though, had the same chocolate-brown eyes.

"Now that I have your attention," Mercy said, lifting her hands and straightening, "I'd like to talk to you." She sat down in the chair in front of the desk. "Whether or not we're going to have this discussion is not up for a vote, by the way."

"You are the bossiest woman I've ever met. You've been married to Tony since Christmas. Have you driven him totally bonkers yet? Poor guy, he probably still hasn't figured out what hit him."

"Don't be silly. Tony is lucky that I chose him as my husband. And he knows that, because I tell him at least once a day." She laughed. "I'm just kidding. We're both aware that we have a beautiful relationship, and we cherish it."

Drew nodded, but didn't speak.

"Okay, Drew, truth time. What's going on with you? At first I decided you were just depressed because you'd broken your wrist, and it's a frustrating nuisance trying to do anything with a cast on. A cast, by the way, which is the grungiest mess I've ever seen."

Drew glanced at the cast and shrugged. "It has character."

"It probably has a disease. Let's get back to the subject."

"Which is?"

"Your behavior since you returned from the wilds of Arizona. I mean, for heaven's sake, it's been four or five weeks now and—"

"Five weeks and two days."

"Who's counting?" Her eyes widened. "*You're* counting. Why are you counting? Because you're eager to get that cast off?"

"We can go with that conclusion."

"Aha! That means there's another reason. Drew, come on, talk to me. I realize you're a more private person than Clark or Phil, and you keep things inside you. You've always done that. None of us have ever pushed you to share until you were ready, but this time I'm going to. I'm not being nosy. I'm very concerned."

"Why?" He tossed the book onto the desk. "I'm useless around here, Mercy. All I can do is answer the phone and customers' questions. I have to do something all day, so I read."

"Read? You're studying, as far as I can see. Big difference there. I've been keeping track of the books you've hauled in here from the library. You've had a stack on horse breeding, ranching, the climate and terrain of Arizona. And today you've got five books on child development. This is not leisure-time fiction. There is definitely something important going on."

He sighed and leaned back in his chair, looking

at Mercy for a long moment. Seeing the love and concern in her eyes, he finally nodded.

"You're right," he said. "It is important, and it would be nice to have someone to discuss it with. Don't say anything to Clark and Phil, though."

"I won't, Drew, but they love you every bit as much as I do."

"I know, and I love them, but you've never been sandwiched between two brothers who excelled at everything they did. I've never talked about this with any of you, but I always felt overshadowed by Phil and Clark. Anything I tried to do, they always did better. Why do you think I took up hiking, camping, all those outdoor activities?"

Mercy frowned. "I guess I never really thought about it."

He sat forward again, crossing his arms on the open book on the desk. "Because, baby sister, neither Clark nor Phil had any interest in that type of thing."

"So you didn't have to compete with them. Oh, Drew, they never meant to show you up."

"I know. And I've found a way to do my own thing and be proud of my achievements. But now . . ." He shook his head.

"Now?"

"Look, you're happily married to Tony. Phil is in Bliss City with Julie and their son. Clark is on a campaign to find a wife, which I know he'll do, because Clark accomplishes every project he undertakes."

"And you?" Mercy asked. "The subject here seems to be relationships, marriage . . . love."

"Bingo. I've had all these weeks to dwell on it. The thing is, Mercy, I'm back in competition with my brothers . . . hell, with the world, and if I blow this, I'd rather no one knew. I was so smug when I left there, but as the days have passed, I'm really shaking in my shorts."

She held up one hand. "Wait. Left there? Arizona? You met a special woman in Arizona?"

"I—I fell in love in Arizona."

"Oh, Drew," she said, smiling warmly, "that's wonderful." Her gaze flickered to the stack of books. "Let me guess. She has a ranch, breeds horses, and either has a child, or you'd like her to have yours. What's her name?"

Drew took a deep breath and let it out slowly. "Memory. Her name is Memory Lawson, and I'm in love with her. She has a five-year-old daughter, Heather, who is as cute as a button, has a thing for Mickey Mouse, and is a miniature Memory."

"I'm so happy for you, Drew."

"Don't be," he said glumly. "Not yet. Memory was hurt very badly by Heather's father, and has a high, thick wall around herself. I've dented it, even gotten through it a few times, but since I've been back here, I've really wondered if I made as much progress as I believed I did."

"If she's there, why are you here?"

"This damn cast, that's why. I grew up in the shadows of two overachiever brothers. It's an even rougher trip to be useless in the eyes of the woman you love, and I have enough strikes against me. My being a member of the male species is a biggie."

"She hates men?"

"Not exactly. Jack, the man she was involved with, was a sleaze, the kind of guy who was out for a good time and wanted no part of responsibility or problems. Memory doesn't trust her own judgment, her ability to tell the good guys from the bad. So, rather than run the risk of being hurt again, she's chosen to go through life alone."

"But you're a wonderful man. You're honest, loyal, thoughtful, you respect women."

He smiled. "You know that and *I* know that, but Memory Lawson is the one I have to convince. Heather is cool. She has me pegged as her daddy, no ifs, ands, or buts about it."

"Smart child."

"Indeed." He frowned again. "I see the doctor tomorrow, Mercy. He's fairly certain that the cast can be removed, judging by the last X ray he took. If it does, I'm telling Phil and Clark that I have to take time off again. That's rotten because I haven't carried my weight since I got back. I don't plan to explain my reasons to them, either."

"Don't worry about that part. Dad will put in some hours here if need be. So, the cast comes off your arm and then what?"

"Then I go to Arizona. I begin the toughest and

most important battle I've fought in my life. Winning the love of Miss Memory Mountain Lawson."

His sister reached across the desk and squeezed his left hand. "Oh, Drew, what can I say?"

"Just hope that you hear angels singing, Mercy."

Memory lay on her back on Memory Mountain, surrounded by a glorious rainbow of fragrant wildflowers. Above her the brilliant blue sky stretched into eternity. Inhaling deeply, she savored the sweet scent of the flowers, and smiled as she heard the symphony being performed by the buzzing bees.

She glanced at Dog, who was fast asleep next to her, then shut her eyes. With her fingers laced on her stomach, she waited for the lovely feeling of peace and contentment she was anticipating to drift over her.

It didn't come.

She wiggled, settled again, and waited.

Every May she came up here to lie among the flowers, enjoy their fragrance, and cherish the peacefulness she'd always found.

This year, though, that peacefulness was elusive, dancing just out of her reach like the butterflies that flitted from flower to flower. And she knew why her treasure hovered beyond her grasp. Drew Sloan.

During the seemingly endless days and nights since he had left, Drew had never been far from her thoughts. He was always there in her mental vision, laughing, smiling, gazing at her warmly, the smoky hue of desire in his eyes.

She could see his naked body, taut, tanned, beautifully proportioned, and fully aroused. She could vividly recall the taste and aroma of his glistening skin. The remembrance of his manhood filling her, consuming her, taking her into blissful oblivion, caused heat to suffuse her.

Lord, how she missed him. There was a void, an emptiness in her life, a place where Drew should be but wasn't, because she'd sent him away.

Memory sighed, but refused to budge or open her eyes. She was going to feel peaceful and contented, darn it, if she had to stay put for two weeks.

That, she thought, was one of the dumbest mental declarations she'd ever made. She was frantically scrambling to regain control of her mind and, heaven help her, her heart.

Drew was gone, and despite what he'd said, he wasn't coming back. Fine. She didn't want him there, gumming up her life, shattering her resolve to never again become involved with a man.

She'd forget Drew . . . in time. The exquisite and precious memories would fade . . . in time. She'd no longer have to avoid addressing the question of whether or not she was in love with him . . . in time.

She opened her eyes.

She might as well admit defeat. Obviously she

was *not* going to obtain her blessed peacefulness and contentment that day. But she would . . . in time. She'd leave the flowers and her private mountain and go for an exhilarating ride on Sugar Shoes.

The beautiful and valuable horse had recovered completely. Lucky Sugar, she thought. Mother Nature had decreed that animals such as that horse wouldn't remember tragic events like the loss of a baby. Sugar Shoes didn't have a broken heart over the death of her foal.

Wise Mother Nature, Memory thought. Human beings caused the angels to be sad enough.

Suddenly, Dog awoke, fully alert. He jumped over Memory where she still lay supine on the ground and growled, the fur on his back standing up in stiff peaks.

She rolled to her feet, grabbing her trusty shotgun. An instant later Dog's growl changed to an excited, happy bark, and his tail wagged rapidly.

"Dog, what— Hey!" She frowned in confusion as the shepherd bounded away, still joyfully barking. "Probably a rabbit," she muttered, cradling the shotgun in both arms.

Then her heart skipped a beat before beginning a wild cadence. Her breath caught, and from somewhere in the recesses of her racing mind, she received a message to remember to breathe. She no longer was aware of the heavy, sweet fragrance of the flowers, nor heard the buzzing of the bees.

She had only one thought that echoed over and over. *Drew Sloan was back.*

He had come up over the rise of the hill and was walking slowly toward her as Dog yipped and yelped in excitement, running circles around him.

Welcome, Drew, her heart murmured.

Go away, Drew, her mind ordered.

Drew was back, her heart answered. Tall and handsome, his thick hair tousled by the breeze and his dark eyes fixed on her. Drew was back.

What nerve, her mind fumed. How dare he just pop up unannounced. And he was trespassing again on her mountain. Well, he could just march his gorgeous self . . .

. . . Right into her arms.

As he came closer, step by step, Memory felt her knees tremble. She could not read the expression on his face, and had absolutely no idea what might be visible on her own.

An amalgam of emotions tumbled through her; joy, fear, anticipation, anger, and desire. Swiftly rising desire.

He stopped in front of her, his gaze locked on hers. Dog flopped onto the ground, his tongue hanging out of the side of his mouth, his tail still wagging.

Say something, Memory told herself. Stop standing there like a star-struck idiot. She had to open her mouth and say something.

"I . . ." she started.

"Shh," Drew said.

He framed her face in his hands and visually traced each of her features. The passion now radiating from his expressive eyes grew more intense with every passing second.

Memory had the rather hysterical thought that her bones were going to melt and she'd dissolve into a puddle at his feet.

Then he lowered his head and kissed her.

Her lashes drifted down, and she parted her lips to eagerly welcome and meet his questing tongue.

Oh, yes, her heart whispered, then all thought was smothered beneath a wave of passion.

Ah, Memory, Drew thought, his heart soaring as he felt her respond to his kiss. He loved her so damn much, and Lord, how he'd missed her.

He wanted to make love to her, there on Memory Mountain, on nature's bed of fragrant wildflowers. He'd join his body with hers, and together they'd be flung into that magical place where ecstasy reined.

At the moment, though, the shotgun she held was poking him in the stomach. *That* was not the type of thing of which romantic interludes were made.

He lifted his head and met her smoky gaze as she slowly raised her lashes. She smiled at him, then stiffened, blinked, and took a quick step backward. He was forced to drop his hands from her face.

"You're . . ." Memory stopped as she became aware that there was no more air in her lungs. She inhaled, exhaled, and tried again. "You're trespassing, Sloan."

He planted his hands on his hips and rolled his eyes. "I can't believe you said that."

"Well, you *are* trespassing."

And she sounded about as old as Heather, she admitted glumly to herself. But she didn't know what to do or say. Her heart was still racing from that sensational kiss, and Drew was so gorgeous, and she was so glad to see him, and she loved him so much, and—

"What?" she said.

"I didn't say anything," he said, "but I will. I'm glad to see you, Memory. Very glad. I missed you."

"I . . . Well, I . . . Oh." She swallowed heavily. She was in love with Drew Sloan? Oh, heaven help her, yes, she was. This was terrible, a disaster. She wasn't going to stand still for this, though. She had no intention of being in love with Drew. But she already was! Oh, Lord, what on earth was she going to do? "Why are you on my mountain?"

He shook his head, smiling wryly. "They'll never recruit you for the welcome wagon, Memory. Look, I'm not trespassing. I drove right to the ranch, had a warm, *kind* welcome from Tina, and she told you were probably up here. She *kindly* urged me to try to find you."

"I see. Well, I guess you're not trespassing, then. You sort of are, but . . . How's your wrist?"

"As good as new. Memory, I know it would have

been more polite for me to have called ahead to check if this was a convenient time to come."

"Good thought."

"But that was too risky. If you told me *not* to come, I'd really be up against it." He shrugged. "So I just came."

"Why?"

"How's Heather? Did she like all the postcards of Mickey Mouse that I sent her?"

"She loved them. She has them on the corkboard in her bedroom. Why are you here?"

"And the ranch? Are things running smoothly?"

"The horses are fine. I'm buried in paperwork that I detest, but there's no solution for that. Rick says I should get a computer. Drew, why are you here?"

"Tina looks great. The kitchen smelled like cinnamon and—"

"Dammit, Sloan, why are you here?"

"Because, Lawson," he yelled right back, "I happen to be in love with you. Have you got that? I . . . love . . . you!" He snapped his mouth closed and sighed. "Scream it in her face, Sloan. That's really beautiful."

She leaned toward him, her cheeks suddenly pale. "I beg your pardon?"

He smiled at her, and his voice was a gentle caress when he spoke.

"I love you. Memory. I love you more than I can even begin to tell you. I came back because I love you, and I intend to do something about it."

"What does that mean?" she asked, a funny little squeak in her voice.

"That I'm going to do everything within my power to convince you that I honestly love you, and at the same time convince you that you honestly love me. You'll see that you *can* trust your judgment, because we're sensational together." He nodded. "That sums it up very nicely, I believe."

"You're crazy," she said. A bubble of laughter escaped from her lips, which she vaguely decided was hysteria breaking free. "You're bonkers, Sloan."

"No," he said thoughtfully, "I'm in love . . . with you."

"I'm not listening to any more of this." She spun around and stalked away. "Come, Dog." The animal trotted after her.

Drew followed, a smug smile tugging at the corners of his mouth.

Memory Lawson was shook, he thought. He'd thrown her for a loop, no doubt about it. She was fighting her feelings for him, but nothing could erase the way she'd responded to his kiss. She cared for him, he was certain of it. The stage was set, the battle begun, and he intended to win. He had to.

The trek down the mountain began in total silence. Drew stayed behind Memory, enjoying again the view of her long legs encased in faded jeans.

Her hiking pace was still off, he mused. She went much too fast, didn't properly gauge the balance between distance and energy. He did not, however, think this was the time to mention that fact.

He'd have to take Heather's training for outdoor activities in hand, that was for sure. He wanted Honey Heather growing up knowing how to do all of it right.

He'd begged for a rest, he recalled, the last time he'd gone down this mountain. But that, of course, was understandable. He'd had a very painful broken wrist.

Today would be no problem. He'd come up this way from the ranch and had made the climb without even breathing hard. Descending was trickier, requiring greater skill to maintain balance, but he'd hiked terrain similar to this a number of times.

One would think, he mused on, that Memory would have figured out, after all the years of climbing her private mountain, that she didn't set her pace properly. Probably she accepted the need to stop and catch her breath, which she'd certainly be doing any second now, as a given.

Ten minutes later Drew registered a sense of déjà vu as he realized that Memory was *not* going to take a break. Also familiar was his own fatigue, with no excuse this time of an injury.

The muscles in his calves were cramping from the sidestepping required to move downward properly. His lungs were beginning to burn. Sweat was trickling down his back, and his throat was parched.

Memory kept on at her steady clip, with Dog bouncing along beside her.

He couldn't believe this, Drew thought incredulously. Memory Lawson was running circles around him. Her pacing wasn't off; it was obviously one that she could easily maintain for whatever distance she chose to cover.

His male ego had just received a tremendous pop in the chops. Memory was a much better hiker than he was, a fact that did not set well with him. For years he'd hoped to find a woman who shared his love of nature's gifts, a partner in likes, a partner for life.

And there she was, Memory Lawson, who could beat the socks off him in the hiking department. No, it wasn't setting well, but by the same token, there was something amusing about it. It served his overblown machismo right to have a comeuppance.

A chuckle rumbled in Drew's chest, then erupted in a full-blown laugh.

Memory stopped and looked back at him, a questioning expression on her face.

"Private joke," he said, grinning.

"Oh," she said, then turned, ready to start off again.

"Memory, wait. I need to catch my breath. Well, you go on. I'll be along in a minute. I know my way to the ranch." He walked to a large rock and sat down, taking a deep breath, then letting it out slowly. "Whew."

Memory stared at him, voices warring in her mind again, telling her to go, telling her to stay. Sighing in defeat, she joined Drew on the rock. She set the shotgun on the ground, and Dog flopped down beside it.

Don't think, she directed herself for the umpteenth time. She would *not* dwell on what Drew had said regarding his feelings for her. She would *not* . . . Oh, who was she kidding? His words were echoing in her mind, beating against her brain and whispering around her heart.

I love you, Memory. I love you more than I can even begin to tell you. I came back because I love you, and I intend to do something about it.

And she loved him. Oh, dear Lord, how she loved him. She'd promised herself that she'd never fall prey to her emotions again, but now there was Drew.

And she was frightened to the very core of her being.

"It sure is pretty up here," he said, bringing her from her tormented reverie. "Those wildflowers are like a carpet spread out as far as the eye can see."

"Yes," said, picking an imaginary speck off her jeans.

"Memory, look at me."

"Are you rested yet?" she asked, her gaze riveted on her knees.

"Look at me."

She slowly raised her head to meet his eyes.

"I'm not going to hurt you," he said, his voice low. "I'm not going to lie to you, or walk away from problems or my responsibilities. I love you, Memory, and I'm asking you to give me, us, a chance."

"No," she whispered. "No."

A moan caught in Drew's throat as he saw the pallor of Memory's skin, the stark fear radiating from her beautiful eyes.

"Memory," he said, his voice raspy with emotion.

He placed one arm across her shoulders and eased her close, nestling her head on his chest. Weaving his fingers through her hair, he kissed the top of her head, inhaling and savoring her aroma of fresh air, soap, and a light scent of flowers.

"Don't cry," he said again.

"I'm not," she mumbled.

Oh, Memory, move, she directed herself wearily. She should pull away, escape from Drew's embrace, march herself down that mountain, and go talk to a horse, a nice, safe, nonthreatening horse.

At that moment, though, she didn't have the physical energy, or the emotional fortitude, to budge. Drew felt so good and smelled so good. He was strong, comforting, and solid. The heat emanating from his body was weaving into hers, chasing away the chill of fear clutching her soul.

That didn't make any sense at all, she thought, since *he* was the cause of her fright. Drew, along with her silent admission that she loved him, was the source of her frantic urge to flee as fast and as far as possible.

"Memory," he said, tightening his hold on her, "I know you were disillusioned in the past, badly hurt, but that was a long time ago. Can't you put it to rest? You're forcing yourself, and me, to pay a price for decisions you made when you were young and very confused."

She jerked back and straightened, forcing him to release her.

"I'm confused now, too, you dolt," she said. "My mind is a mess, my life is in chaos, and dammit, it's all your fault."

He smiled. "That's good news. I'd hate to think I wasn't having any impact on you."

"Oh, you're infuriating." She folded her arms beneath her breasts and glared at him.

"Me?" he said, splaying one hand on his chest. "No I'm not. I'm a very nice person, who happens to be deeply in love with you."

"Quit saying that!"

He squinted up at the sky for a long moment, giving the impression that he was contemplating her order. When he looked at her again, he was still smiling.

"Sorry," he said. "I consider myself a cooperative, easy-to-get-along-with kind of guy, but I just can't go with that command . . . I mean, request. If I didn't tell you that I love you, it would bottle up inside me and probably blow a gasket."

He shrugged and lifted his hands in a gesture of "What can I do?" "That's a fact, ma'am. You'll get used to hearing it. Oh, and feel free to say you love me whenever the urge strikes."

"That does it." She jumped to her feet. Dog attempted to follow suit so quickly, he toppled onto his nose and yelped. "I'm not having this conversation with you, Sloan."

"Whatever you say, Lawson." He stood up. "Shall we go?"

She glowered at him once more for good measure, snatched up the shotgun, then spun around and strode away. They finished the descent from Memory Mountain in complete silence.

When they reached the flat stretch of land leading to the ranch house, Drew fell into step beside her.

"I want to assure you," he said seriously, "that I won't say anything regarding my feelings for you in front of Heather. This is between you and me, and involving Heather wouldn't be fair."

Memory sighed. "Your coming back has involved Heather. Every time one of your postcards arrived, she'd go on an I-want-Drew-to-be-my-daddy tangent. When she gets home from school and sees you, she'll no doubt believe it's *fait accompli*."

"Oh. Well, I won't reinforce that notion."

"Dandy," she said dryly. "How can I ever thank you?" She paused. "Where, pray tell, do you think you're staying during this little visit of yours?"

"I brought all of my camping gear. I mean, really, Memory, I'm not so crass that I'd arrive unannounced and expect you to put me up as though you were running a hotel."

"That's comforting."

"But when I told Tina that I was going to camp out, she fussed and fumed, got that Italian temper of hers in a rip. She wasn't hearing of me sleeping out on the ground. So . . ." He slid a glance at Memory. ". . . I'm back in the room I had when I was here before. Don't blow a fuse, Memory, you'll stress yourself out."

"And just how long are we to be blessed with your presence, Mr. Sloan?" she asked, no hint of a smile on her face.

He shrugged. "For as long as it takes, darlin'. I've come to woo and win you."

"Oh, for crying out loud. This is absurd."

"There is nothing absurd about my being in love with you."

She stopped and faced him, the shotgun once again cradled in her arms.

"Drew, this is ridiculous," she said wearily. "Suppose that I . . . that we . . . which isn't going to happen . . . but just suppose . . ."

"That you admitted that you love me?"

"I'm speaking, so you listen."

"Yes, ma'am."

"Even if we were . . . together, it wouldn't work. You live in Santa Barbara and are part of a family business you're committed to. I would never give up this ranch and my lifestyle. This is where I belong, and where I intend to stay. Have you bothered to think about details like that?"

"Of course I have. I'm not a dunce, you know. I have it all figured out."

"Do tell." She shook her head, and began to walk again.

"No, I won't 'do tell.' Not right now. You're not in a receptive mood. We'll cover all the nitty-gritty details later."

She wanted to cover them now, darn it, Memory thought. She had enough natural curiosity to wish to hear how the oh-so-brilliant Mr. Sloan had managed to make a totally impossible situation possible.

Forget it, she thought in the next instant. To pursue the issue would give the impression that she was weakening in her resolve not to acknowledge what was happening between them.

No, he could keep his nitty-gritty details to himself. He was dangling the plan in front of her, just out of reach, creating a multitude of unanswered questions in her mind.

But Mr. Smug Sloan was in for a long wait, because it would be a very cold day in a very hot place before she asked him one blasted nitty-gritty thing.

Eight

By seven-thirty that evening Memory had mentally moved from punching Drew in the nose to strangling him with her bare hands.

He was driving her right up the wall. Ticking off his offenses on imaginary fingers, sounded, even to herself, absolutely ridiculous. She could not—unless she wished to be carted to the funny farm—call Drew on the carpet for his behavior.

She would seem like a blithering idiot if she pitched a fit because Drew was sitting on the sofa, a pajama-clad Heather tucked beside him as he read her a story.

Nor would she appear even remotely sane for being irritated as all get-out that Drew had been a perfect gentleman at dinner, engaging both her and Heather in fascinating conversation.

He had handled the reunion with Heather with

finesse, smoothly avoiding her question of whether he'd come back so that he could be her daddy. He'd returned for a "Heather hug," he'd announced, then lifted her up and swung her around until the little girl was squealing in delight.

He had not, Memory admitted, stared lasciviously at her, nor slipped any sexual innuendos over Heather's head to land in her lap.

No, she would be hard put to list Drew's offenses that had pushed her to the point of simmering fury, had stretched her nerves to a taut limit. He had not, in actuality, done anything wrong.

Except for being there!

And was he ever *there.* His mere presence seemed to fill the room to overflowing. She was acutely aware of each move he made, each smile that lit up his face, each glance he sent her way.

His blatant masculinity seemed to pour over her, into her, until her entire body ached for his touch. Passion flamed within her, desire in its purest form.

She loved him.

Oh, how she yearned to fling herself into his arms and declare her love, announce that she'd overcome her fears and was ready, willing, and able to return his love.

But she couldn't, and along with her unreasonable anger was an ever-growing sadness. She was held fast in a cold fist created by the pain of the past, and was unable to break free.

She had to be strong, Memory thought. She mustn't listen to Drew's declarations of love, mustn't succumb to the magnetism of the man himself.

She would not reveal her true feelings for him, as it would render her totally vulnerable. She would have nothing left with which to protect herself should it turn out that she had once again chosen the wrong man to give her heart to.

"The end," Drew said, snapping the book closed.

Memory jumped as the sudden noise brought her abruptly from her tangled thoughts.

"Read me another story," Heather said. "Please, Drew? Pretty please."

Memory got to her feet. "No more stories tonight, Heather. It's your bedtime, sweetheart. Come on, sleepy girl, and I'll tuck you in."

Heather slid off the sofa, then turned and grasped Drew's right hand with both of hers.

"You come, too, Drew," she said. "I want you to tuck me in too."

"Well," he said, looking up at Memory, "we'd better ask your mom if it's all right."

"Mommy?"

"Yes, of course," Memory said. "Drew can help tuck you in."

In her room, which was decorated in pink and white dotted swiss, Heather tugged on Drew's hand, urging him to cross the room to where a corkboard hung on the wall.

"See, Drew?" she said. "All the pictures of Mickey

Mouse you sent me are here. I stuck them with pushpins. Do you know what pushpins are? You gotta have pushpins for a corkboard, you know. Now let me show you my cards of Mickey Mouse. I fixed them real nice 'cause—"

"Stalling," Memory said in a singsong voice. She smiled at Heather. "Into bed, madam, as quick as a bunny. Drew has seen the postcards because he's the one who sent them to you, remember?"

Heather sighed dramatically. "But maybe he forgot what they looked like, Mommy."

Drew chuckled. "Forget Mickey Mouse? Never happen, Honey Heather. Jump into bed."

After a trip to the bathroom, then another for a drink of water, Heather was at last settled in bed. Memory kissed her, straightened the covers, then kissed her again. She stepped back to allow Drew to take her place.

"Good night, Honey Heather," he said, and leaned over and kissed her on the forehead. "Sleep tight and don't let the bedbugs bite."

Heather giggled, then frowned.

"Are you going to be my daddy?" she asked. "I asked you before, but you didn't tell me. Are you? Are you going to be my daddy?"

You betcha, Memory thought dreamily. They'd be a family, the three of them. The house would be filled with the sound of angels singing, because everyone would be so happy and . . . Oh, Memory, shut up.

"We'll talk about that another time," Drew said.

"You close those beautiful dark eyes and go to sleep. Maybe you'll dream about Mickey Mouse."

"Oh, that would be fun." Heather squeezed her eyes closed. "Maybe Minnie Mouse will be in my dreams too."

"There you go," Drew said. "Good night."

A minute later Memory and Drew reentered the living room. Drew sat down on the sofa and watched Memory fiddle with the books in the bookcase, straightening what was already neat as a pin.

"You seem edgy tonight, Memory."

"Me?" she said quickly, not looking at him. "No, no, not at all. I'm fine, just fine."

"Are you sure?"

"Oh, yes, I'm positive."

"Well, that's good, because I'd hate to ask you what I'm about to ask you if you weren't totally together."

She turned and looked at him. "Ask away," she said, waving one hand in the air. "What's on your tiny mind?"

Drew gazed at her for a long moment, then finally said, "Memory, will you marry me?"

Her eyes widened and her mouth dropped open. She stared at Drew as though she'd never seen him before in her life.

He smiled. "Doing an impersonation of a goldfish when you've just been proposed to really isn't very romantic."

She snapped her mouth closed and sank onto

the nearest chair, her trembling legs refusing to hold her for another second. Her heart was beating wildly.

"Will I . . ." she started, her voice wobbly. "That's not funny, Drew."

His smile disappeared and he leaned forward, resting his elbows on his knees.

"I'm not attempting to be humorous. I've never been more serious about anything in my life. I love you, Memory, and I want us to spend the rest of our lives together."

"You do not."

He dropped his chin to his chest for a second, then looked at her again.

"Lord, you're difficult to deal with."

"Then don't deal with me," she shot back. "Just pack up and shuffle off to Santa Barbara."

"Is that what you want?" He planted his hands on his thighs and pushed himself to his feet. "Do you want me to leave, with the promise to never come back?"

He started toward her, slowly, so slowly, his eyes riveted on hers. Memory pressed back against the chair, the rapid thudding of her heart echoing in her ears.

"Say it, Memory. Tell me to go." He continued to advance toward her. "Can you honestly do that? Can you look directly at me as you're doing now and say, 'Drew Sloan, I don't want you, don't desire you, I feel nothing whatsoever for you, so exit stage left and don't darken my doorway again'?"

He stopped in front of her and leaned down to grip the arms of the chair, trapping her in place, caging her with his body.

"Can you say all that, Memory?"

She pressed even harder against the back of the chair, unable to tear her gaze from Drew's. His big powerful body loomed over her, and the heat emanating from him seemed to weave from him to her. Staring at him, she felt as though she were drowning in the depths of his eyes.

Not want him, not desire him? Dear Lord, she *ached* with the need of him, was awash with passion's fire that was throbbing with a maddening pulse deep within her.

Feel nothing whatsoever for him? She was irrevocably in love with him. Tell him to go and never come back? Oh, no. A future without Drew evoked images of chilling darkness with no hint of warm sunshine, of long, lonely days and longer nights.

She yearned to reach up and frame his face with her hands, urge his mouth onto hers to share a searing kiss that would fan the flames of desire within them.

She wanted to make love with Drew, and *declare* her love, announce it to him and the world.

But no words would come. Her fear was a mighty foe, her self-doubt a menacing force.

"Memory?"

"Drew, please, don't. Just don't."

"Listen to me," he said. "I love you and I want to marry you. I'll be the daddy Heather wishes me to be, and love her and the children we'll create together totally and equally."

He straightened and took a step back, making it possible for her to flee. She didn't move.

"I realize," he went on, "that I'm dumping an awful lot on you all at once. Maybe that's a mistake, but I don't think so. You don't trust your own judgment in regard to men, and the bottom line is that you therefore don't trust *me.*"

He dragged a hand through his hair. "So I'm laying it all out for you. I'm not playing games here, Memory. I'm talking about the rest of our lives, our entire future. When you come to believe what I've just said, you will have escaped, at last, from the past and will believe in yourself too. Then, and only then, can we move forward together."

He took a deep breath and let it out slowly.

"I'll wait for you, Memory," he said, his voice raspy with emotion. "I realize that you're frightened. But I intend to fight for you, for us. I'm going to tell you over and over how much I love you. I'm going to ask you again and again to marry me. *You are my life, Memory Lawson.*"

"Oh, God," she said, covering her face with her hands. A sob caught in her throat.

"Angels singing?" he said quietly. "Or angels sad? It's up to you. Good night, Memory." He turned and strode from the room.

And Memory gave way to her threatening tears.

• • •

The next day dawned clear and warm. The sky was dotted with white fluffy clouds, and the sweet aroma of wildflowers mingled with the scents of the ranch. It was an invigorating day, nature at its best, creating a feeling that all was right with the world.

Except for one thing.

Drew Sloan was having his first lesson in how to ride a horse.

"Oh, hell," he said, for the sixth time. "I did it again."

Franco shook his head and chuckled, the wiry little Italian having long since given up any attempt to hide his amusement. He walked to the horse that Drew was perched on, retrieved the reins that were trailing on the ground, and handed them back to Drew.

"Drew," he said, "think of the reins as the steering wheel. You can't let go of the steering wheel every two minutes."

"I know, I know," Drew said, "but there's just so much to remember, and all of a sudden . . . I'll tell you something, Franco. This saddle is not what I would call comfortable. My respect for John Wayne just went up another couple of notches."

Franco hooted with laughter. Drew glared at him.

"You're about to have an audience," Franco

said, grinning. "Memory and Heather just left the house and are headed this way."

"Oh, hell."

"Okay, here we go," Franco said. "Nudge him with your heels. Easy does it."

Drew did as instructed, and the horse started forward at a lazy walk. Drew clutched the saddle horn with both hands, managing to hold onto the reins at the same time. The horse plodded along the inside edge of the corral, turning corners on his own. Drew just kept holding on for dear life.

"Hi, Drew," Heather called as she and Memory reached the corral. "Whatcha doin'?"

"Scaring myself to death," he said. "This is one very tall horse, Honey Heather. There's a mile between where I'm sitting up here and that very hard ground down there. But I'll get the hang of this . . . in ten or twenty years. Drew Sloan doesn't give up."

Nor did he play fair, Memory thought. He was learning to ride a horse because horses were a major part of her world. He was setting aside his pride, running the risk of appearing foolish in front of her, Heather, and Franco.

Oh, Drew, I love you.

She'd spent a restless night dozing, then awakening to hear Drew's words echoing yet again in her mind.

Memory, will you marry me? You are my life, Memory Lawson.

What more did she want? she asked herself.

Everything, *everything*, Drew said and did told her he was being honest and sincere.

The man she loved, loved her.

The man she loved wished to spend the rest of his life with her.

The man she loved had asked her to marry him.

It was storybook perfect, but . . .

But she was still frightened.

It was hopeless, all of it. She loved Drew, but she lacked the courage to tell him. She wanted to marry him, but he'd never know.

"That's it for today," he said. "My . . ." He glanced at Heather. "My posterior is registering major complaints."

Franco halted the horse, and Drew got off with less-than-graceful form.

"Oh, Lord," he said, with a groan. "Whose dumb idea was this?"

"Same time tomorrow, Drew?" Franco asked.

"Yeah, I'll be here. I'm bound to get better at this, because I doubt that anyone could do it worse."

"Heather," Franco said, "come help me tend to Sailor here, then we'll get you up on Ralph."

"Yes, yes," Heather said, and ran to meet Franco at the gate to the corral.

Drew climbed over the fence to stand next to Memory.

"Madam," he said, "you have just witnessed Olympic-potential horsemanship."

"Oh, is that what that was?" she said, smiling.

"Indeed. I'll figure out this horse-riding thing, though."

Her smile faded. "Why?"

"Why? Because horses are important to you, and that makes them important to me. I studied stacks of books on horses, ranching, the whole nine yards, while I was waiting for my wrist to mend. I take what you do here very seriously, Memory. I love you, remember?"

"But what about *your* career?"

"I did a lot of research in that area too. That falls under the nitty-gritty details I wanted to discuss with you. I guess this is a good time to cover them. You were too crabby before." He leaned toward her, his eyes narrowed as he scrutinized her face. "You're not crabby at the moment, are you?"

She laughed. "No."

"Good. Let's go for a walk."

They strolled away from the corral. Their destination, she realized a few minutes later, was the open expanse of flat grassy land between the ranch and Memory Mountain. When they arrived in the center of the meadow. Drew stopped.

"Okay, here goes," he said, turning to face her. "I studied more than horses during those weeks. I want to learn to ride so we can do it together. I also want to learn about breeding horses, because it's what you do. I would not, however, attempt to tell you how to conduct your business."

"Go on," she said.

"You asked me about *my* career. Well, I can put it to use here, if you agree. I know you'll never leave this ranch, so I've got to adapt my area of expertise to"—he swept one arm through the air—"your turf."

She looked at him intently, but didn't speak.

"This stretch of land is perfect," he went on. "I checked it thoroughly, talked to experts, and it works. It can be done right here."

"What can be done?"

"Pecan trees, Memory," he said, his eyes sparkling. "You raise your horses, and I'll grow the best pecans in the West. That's the nitty-gritty, the way we blend our lives."

"Pecan trees," she said slowly. "You're right, they are grown in this area. I've never considered it because I have enough to do, but there's a rancher about ten miles from here who grows them. You really did research all this, didn't you?"

He nodded and took her hands in his. His voice was low when he spoke again, his expression tender.

"Don't you see, Memory? There's nothing standing in our way except your fears." He lowered his head and brushed his lips over hers. She shivered from the feathery kiss. "Nothing."

She blinked, cleared her throat, and took a step back. "Now wait," she said. "Yes, pecan trees would work in this meadow. But Drew, there's more than that to consider."

"Like what?"

"Life on this ranch. You're from the city, you're accustomed to having all the things that city living offers. It's isolated here, Drew. There are no movies, shopping malls, sports events. You don't really know that you'd be contented here."

He frowned. "Of course I would. Lord, Memory, *you'd* be here. You're the woman I love, the one I want to spend the rest of my life with. Do you really think Santa Barbara holds any appeal for me when I imagine being there without you? Hell, no, it doesn't. I want to be with you and Heather."

"Now," she said, throwing up her hands. "That's what you want right now, at this point in time." She shook her head. "But how long will you feel this way? What happens when you get restless, bored, become angry when you think about all you gave up to be here? Tell me, Drew, what happens to us then?"

He planted his hands on his hips and stared up at the sky for a moment, attempting to control his rising temper. He puffed out his cheeks and expelled a long breath, then looked at Memory again.

"Why are you doing this?" There was a sharp edge to his voice despite his efforts to tamp down his temper. "You're knocking yourself out to find something wrong with my plan, inventing problems that we don't even have."

"No I'm not," she said, her voice rising. "I'm trying to be realistic, Drew. I can't put on rose-

colored glasses and see no further than you growing pecan trees while I'm tending to my horses."

"Why the hell not? It's a solution, a damn fine
one, as to how we can make us, together, work.
Why can't you go with that?"

"Trust in my judgment? Make a conscious decision to throw caution to the wind, go for the
gusto, not look closely at the big picture, the
long-term future? Dear Lord, Drew, that would be
so foolish of me."

She blinked away threatening tears, telling herself that she absolutely, positively, *would not cry.*

"And when it all falls apart?" she went on. "I'll
have only myself to blame . . . again. I'll be alone,
and lonely. I'll have to face the fact that I once
again chose the wrong man to love, to give my
heart to . . ." She shook her head as tears choked
off her words.

Drew stared at her, then slowly a smile tugged
at his lips, finally broadening into a grin.

Memory crossed her arms and lifted her chin. "I
do not, Mr. Sloan, find this discussion humorous."

"I'm not laughing. This is pure, unadulterated
joy you're witnessing, Ms. Lawson."

She narrowed her eyes. "You're weird."

"Nope. I'm in love and . . ." He punched one fist
high in the air. "All right!" he yelled.

Surprised at his sudden outburst, Memory took
a step backward. He immediately closed the distance between them and gripped her shoulders.

"You didn't listen to your own words, **Memory**," he said. "But I did. Oh, yes, I heard exactly what you said."

"What—"

"You said," he interrupted, "that you love me, that you've given your heart to me."

"I did not say one thing about . . ." She stopped speaking and stared up at him. "Oh. Yes, I did."

He shifted his hands from her shoulders to her face. "Yes . . ." He flicked his tongue over her lips. ". . . you . . ." He kissed the tip of her nose. ". . . did."

His mouth melted over hers, his tongue parting her lips to meet her tongue. He dropped his hands from her face and encircled her with his arms, nestling her close, molding her against him.

Of their own volition, it seemed, Memory's arms floated upward to entwine around Drew's neck, her fingers sinking into his thick, silky hair. Her lashes drifted down, and rational thought fled as she savored the taste, the feel, of Drew.

Her breasts were crushed to the hard wall of his chest, creating a tantalizing pain and evoking images of Drew's hands and lips soothing the soft flesh. His arousal was full and heavy, and she pressed against him, causing a groan of desire to rumble in his throat.

Heat churned low in her body, pulsing in the same seductive rhythm as his tongue dueling with hers. When he slid his hands over her buttocks and fitted her more snugly into the cradle of his hips, she nearly dragged him down to the ground.

Memory loved him, Drew thought hazily. She was in love with him, had given her heart to him. The victory he sought in his battle to win her love for all time was definitely, wondrously close.

But he knew Memory was still fighting back, her fears giving her strength. She seemed determined to undermine the plans he presented for their future, scrambling to find fault with his solution as to how they could mesh their two worlds. But he was determined too. *Nothing* would destroy what he and Memory had. He loved her beyond reason, beyond having words to describe the depths of that love. And Memory loved *him*. They were going to have it all. Forever.

He lifted his head a fraction of an inch to speak close to her lips.

"I love you," he said, his voice gritty with passion, "and you love me. That's who we are, what we have together, the foundation we'll build our future on. We're unbeatable, Memory. Nothing can defeat us. Nothing." He brushed his lips over hers. "Please say it, Memory. Tell me you love me."

"I love you, Drew Sloan," she said dreamily, her eyes only half open. "I love you."

Moaning, he lowered her to the thick carpet of sweet grass, his body partially covering hers as he kissed her.

Memory was floating in a sensual mist, aware

only of her own body and every inch of Drew's. She was on fire, burning with the need for him to possess her, thrust deep within her and carry them both up and away to their heavenly place of ecstasy.

Yes, she loved him, and now he knew. And yes, she wanted him, and that he knew. Nothing could defeat them, he had said. The future was theirs. He would grow his pecan trees there in the meadow and . . .

A chill swept through her, causing her to shiver and whisking away passion's heated haze.

Grow his pecan trees, she mentally repeated, and grow restless and bored on the isolated ranch. If Drew stayed, she'd spend her days watching, waiting, for signs of his discontentment.

She would live in fear, fear of his leaving, fear of having to face yet again that she had chosen the wrong man to love, fear that when she began to cry, she'd never be able to stop.

No!

She pushed against his shoulders, forcing him away as she tore her mouth from his.

"No," she said.

"I want you," he said in a hoarse whisper. "You want me, too, I know you do. We'll make love here, in this place, our place. This is where I'll grow my pecan trees. This land is what will intertwine our worlds after we're married. Let me love you, Memory, here."

"No," she said, pressing harder on his shoulders. "Get off me, Drew. Leave me alone."

Drew frowned. She saw anger flicker across his face, followed by hurt that settled in his eyes. He moved off her, and she struggled to her feet, praying her trembling legs would hold her. He rose to stand in front of her.

She refused to meet his gaze, the pain and confusion in his eyes, knowing that she had caused it. She folded her arms tightly beneath her breasts as though she were holding herself together. She stared unseeing at the center of Drew's chest.

"I love you, Drew," she said. "I can't deny that. But it doesn't matter, because I won't allow it to. I won't marry you, Drew, or talk, dream, about our future together. I can't."

He gripped her shoulders and gave her a small shake. "Don't do this. Don't give in to your fears, Memory. Let the past go, believe in me, trust me. Dear Lord, Memory, don't throw us away. We *do* have a future together, until death parts us. Can't you see that? Don't do this to us. Memory, please, put your ghosts to rest. Marry me. Say it, now, tell me you'll be my wife, the mother of my children."

She jerked free of his hold. "No." She took one, then two, steps backward. "No! I want you to leave me alone. I can't. I—I just can't. Drew, please . . . just leave me alone."

She turned and ran, stumbling, nearly blinded by the tears filling her eyes.

Drew lifted one hand toward her in an empty

gesture, a futile attempt to keep her with him. His hand fell heavily to his side. He took a ragged breath, then stared up at the heavens as he strove to control his raging emotions.

But he couldn't see the brilliant blue sky past the tears shimmering in his eyes.

Nine

To Memory it seemed to take an eternity to cross the meadow and reach the corral that was the farthest from the barn.

She leaned her back against the wooden fence, gasping for breath and frantically trying to stop the tears that cascaded down her cheeks. She wrapped her hands around her elbows in a protective gesture and closed her eyes.

Oh, Drew, I'm sorry. So very sorry. She'd hurt him, seen the pain in his beautiful eyes. She had seen it, and she'd never forget it.

Drink a toast to fear, she thought miserably. Declare it the mighty victor that refused to relinquish its cold grip on her soul. It held her with an ironlike fist, unwilling to release her from the dark shadows of the past so she might move into the sunshine of the future with Drew.

She shook her head as fresh tears caused an ache in her throat. She swept her trembling hands roughly over her pale cheeks, determined to stop the senseless crying that was accomplishing nothing.

Turning, she folded her arms on top of the fence and rested her chin on them. Taking a deep breath, she inhaled the familiar scents of the ranch.

But something was missing . . . the unique and special aroma of Drew.

She listened, hearing the chorus of nature, horses whinnying in the distance and the faint tinkling laughter of her daughter.

But something was missing . . . the rich timbre of Drew's voice and the sound of his laughter.

She lifted her head and swept her troubled gaze over all that was within her view, the land, the buildings, and animals, which were only a part of what her beloved ranch offered her.

But something was missing . . . the sight of magnificently masculine Drew Sloan, the man she loved.

The man she'd lost.

With a weary, sad sigh, she moved away from the corral, heading for the house. She'd go around to the front door, she decided, before Heather saw her and called to her to come watch her riding Ralph.

She couldn't face anyone now; she'd dissolve into a weepy mess if someone even spoke to her.

Worse yet was the realization that she was unable to face, to tolerate or forgive, herself.

She was a coward, not strong enough to break free of the clutches of the past. With no one to blame but herself, she was sentenced to a bleak and lonely future without Drew.

At the house Memory carefully opened the front door, not wishing to alert Tina to the fact that she had entered. She closed the door behind her and tiptoed toward the hallway leading to her bed-room. She turned the corner and bumped into Tina, who was wielding a bright pink feather duster.

"Oh!" Memory said. "I'm sorry. I didn't see you. I'm really sorry."

"Yes," Tina said, frowning as she looked at Memory, "I imagine it's difficult to see clearly with eyes puffy from crying."

"Crying?" Memory strove for an expression of innocence that didn't materialize. "Who's crying? *I'm* certainly not crying. Heavenly days, no, I've— I've never been happier."

And with that, Memory burst into tears.

Tina pointed the feather duster down the hall. "To your room, Memory Lawson. Right now."

Memory did as instructed, sniffling all the way. In her room, she sank onto the bed. Tina plunked a box of tissues onto her lap, then sat down next to her. Memory pulled a tissue free and dabbed at her nose.

"I'm crying," she said, then hiccuped.

Tina nodded. "With vigor. So, what went wrong between you and Drew?"

"I don't recall mentioning his name," she said, lifting her chin.

"My dear child," Tina said gently, "tears like that don't come from stubbing your toe. Those are tears from the heart, and your heart holds Drew Sloan. Now, talk to your Tina."

"I love him," Memory said, though it was more in the form of a wail.

"Yes, I know that. Go on."

"And I . . . I . . . I've lost him because I'm too frightened of loving him. I fought the battle against those fears, but I just . . . can't . . ." She stopped speaking as tears choked off her words. She pressed the tissue to her nose.

"Oh, Memory, Memory," Tina said, patting her knee. "How can you allow what happened over five years ago dictate your entire future? Drew loves you, and he loves Heather."

"I know, but I'm so scared, Tina. Drew wants to marry me and live here so I can stay on the ranch. He has a plan to grow pecan trees in the meadow below Memory Mountain. He's willing to give up everything he has in Santa Barbara for me."

"Drew loves you," Tina repeated firmly. "He's coming into the world of the woman he loves."

"But for how long? He'll get bored, discontented. He'll find reasons to leave me. He will, Tina. I can't do this, I just can't. Not only would my heart be shattered, but so would Heather's. It's too risky."

"Fine," Tina said, getting to her feet. "Then send Drew away, tell him to go." She crossed the room to the door, then stopped and turned. "But know this, Memory Lawson. Because of your fears, you will have sentenced yourself, your child, all of us, to live in a house where no angels are singing."

Memory hung her head. "I can't help it, Tina," she mumbled.

Tina looked at her for a long moment, and her voice was soft and gentle when she spoke again.

"Can't you? Look deep within your heart for your strengths, Memory. The battle is over only if you say it is."

Memory continued to sit on the bed after Tina had left, not having the energy to move. She lost track of time as she remained alone in the quiet room, lost in her tormented thoughts.

After pacing back and forth across the room during the half hour he'd been talking, Drew stopped in front of where Rick Sanchez sat behind a wobbly wooden desk.

"There you have it," Drew said, dragging one hand through his hair, "the whole gruesome tale." He shook his head. "I'm telling you, Rick, I was on top of the world when Memory told me that she loved me, then—bam—she cut me off at the knees. I've done everything I can possibly think of to convince her that we're real, we can make it together, have it all. I fought hard, gave it everything I had, but dammit to hell, I lost."

The frown that had formed on Rick's face deepened.

"If she said that she loves you," Rick said, "then she loves you."

"Oh, I don't doubt that she does," Drew said, throwing up his hands. "But her fears are bigger, stronger, than that love. My ball game is over, and I was called out on strikes. There's nothing more I can do or say, Rick."

"Listen, I—"

"Lord," Drew went on, staring up at the ceiling for a long moment, "I'm totally bummed out." He looked at Rick again. "I have never before in my life felt so frustrated, angry, sad . . . Hell, I'm miserable."

Rick smacked the desk hard with the palm of one hand, lunging to his feet at the same time. Drew jerked in surprise.

"Then, dammit, man," Rick yelled, "do something about it."

"Like what, genius?" Drew hollered.

Rick opened his mouth to snap back an answer, then closed it again.

"Hell," he said, shrugging. "I don't know."

Drew slouched in the chair opposite the desk. Rick sank back into his chair. Both frowning, the two men stared into space, and a heavy, gloomy silence hung over the room.

• • •

The next morning Memory rode Sugar Shoes across the ranch land, relishing the feel of the wind in her face. She and the sleek horse moved in harmony, nearly one entity.

The night had been long as she'd tossed and turned, replaying in her mind that final scene in the meadow with Drew. She hadn't seen him since; he'd telephoned from Rick's telling Tina he wouldn't be at the ranch for dinner.

Memory had heard him come in well after midnight, and she'd yearned to rush into his embrace, kiss him senseless, lead him to her bed, and share exquisite lovemaking through the remaining hours of the night.

But she hadn't moved, and the sound of his bedroom door shutting had prompted fresh tears to fill her eyes.

Angels singing, angels sad, Memory thought, as Sugar thundered on, racing the wind. Both Drew and Tina had placed the responsibility of the angels in her lap. She alone had the future of so many lives in her hands.

As the meadow below Memory Mountain came into view, she slowed Sugar Shoes to a walk. In the center of the grassy expanse she pulled on the reins to stop the horse.

Again the heartbreaking exchange that had taken place there with Drew replayed in her mind. And again she felt the ache of tears close her throat.

Her gaze swept over the land, imagining rows of pecan trees nurtured by Drew's attention and skill. To turn that meadow into a prosperous grove would be a tremendous challenge, one Drew would give his maximum effort to.

Whatever Drew did, he gave it his all. There were no half measures about Drew Sloan, whether he was working or playing.

Memory stiffened in the saddle, causing Sugar Shoes to shift restlessly beneath her.

"And loving?" she whispered.

Yes, she thought. And loving.

With her heart racing as fast as her thoughts, Memory nearly forgot to breathe as the tangle in her mind began to sift and sort into order.

"Dear heaven," she finally said aloud, "what have I done? Oh, God, Drew, what have I done?"

With a flick of the reins, she set Sugar Shoes into motion, the powerful horse leaping forward, carrying Memory swiftly back home.

As Memory walked toward the back of the house, she saw Heather and Tina in the distance. As planned, the pair was planting seeds in the freshly turned soil of the garden area.

Upon entering the kitchen, Memory stopped, straining to hear anything that would give evidence to Drew being in the house. There was only silence.

She closed her eyes and took a steadying breath.

Then, with her shoulders squared and her chin lifted, she went in search of Drew.

At the open doorway to his bedroom she stopped, her heart thudding painfully as she saw what he was doing. He was packing his belongings into his duffel bag.

No! she cried silently. She had to talk to him, she had to tell him . . .

"Drew?"

He stiffened but did not turn. After a momentary stillness he continued with his task.

"Yes?" he said quietly.

"You're leaving."

"Yes."

No! "Drew, I'd like to talk to you."

"Go ahead." He stuffed a shirt into the bag.

Memory walked into the room, her legs as wobbly as jelly.

What she said in the next few minutes, she knew, would determine her entire future. She would soon know if she was destined to be alone and lonely, or if that house would be a home filled with the litany of singing angels.

She halted about three feet away from Drew and wrapped her hands around her elbows.

"Drew, I love you."

He nodded. "I know." A pair of tennis shoes went into the bag.

"I—I rode Sugar Shoes this morning, and went to the meadow where you plan to grow the pecan trees."

"Planned. Past tense."

"Drew, I . . . Would you please stop packing and listen to me?"

He sighed, the weary sound seeming to come from his very soul. When he straightened and faced her, she saw the fatigue on his face.

"Listen to you?" he repeated, his voice flat. "No, I really don't want to hear it all again, Memory. What's the point? I love you, you love me, but it isn't enough. With all the space and power you allow your fears to have, nothing would be enough."

"Drew, please, let me have my say."

He folded his arms over his chest. "Go ahead."

She swallowed heavily, then forced herself to meet his gaze. "I've been terribly confused and frightened, Drew," she began. Her voice grew steadier with each word she spoke. "But as I sat there on Sugar Shoes in that meadow, things started to fall into place."

He didn't speak; his face was expressionless.

"I realized my emotional measuring stick regarding loving people and being in love had stopped in time. It was based on the experiences I had when I lost my parents, then later in my relationship with Jack.

"My mother and father were here, then suddenly they were gone. I was with Jack, but the moment I represented a problem to him, it was over and I was alone again. If something was not to his liking, he dismissed it by either ignoring it or walking away."

"I'm not that man," Drew said.

"I know that, but a part of me, the fearful part, equated loving with losing, with being terribly hurt. I kept seeing obstacles in our path that would cause you to leave me.

"I now know that because I shared my inner feelings with you about my parents' death, I've finally said a gentle farewell to them. It was something I should have done years ago.

"But with you and me, I was still frightened of running the risk of loving you. The pain I experienced with Jack was all I knew about loving a man, and I assumed that that kind of heartache would happen again.

"You have every right to be angry and hurt, Drew. I don't have enough words available to me to tell you how sorry I am."

She paused as her voice began to tremble.

"But this morning in the meadow I finally realized how you give everything you do your maximum effort. If you truly believe in it, you give it your all, be it work, play, or—or love."

He nodded, interest beginning to glow in his eyes.

"It was suddenly so clear," she went on. "I had to go far into the imaginary future to find the problem that would cause you to walk away. Why? Why did I do that, look for a problem so far ahead in time?"

"Good question," he said. "And the answer? Did you find it?"

"Yes. Oh, Drew, it was because in the present and the near future we *have* no problems or obstacles to overcome. You don't walk away from problems. You plow right into the middle of them and get them squared away. I was so busy clinging to my fears, I didn't see the effort, the giving, that your solving those problems meant."

"What exactly are you saying?"

"Oh, Drew, I'm so sorry I was so foolish. When I built those walls around my heart, I rendered myself unable to grow as a woman. You were the recipient of the irrational thinking of a child. I know now that if you get restless, we'll fix it. And we'll take Heather to Disneyland to meet Mickey Mouse."

"Memory?" Drew said, hardly breathing.

"Drew, forgive me. Please? Marry me, Drew. Please? I love you, want to be your wife, your partner, your other half. I want Heather to have you for a daddy, and grow up with the children you and I will create together. Oh, Drew, I want this home to overflow with the sound of angels singing."

Drew attempted to speak, but had to clear his throat as his emotions raged beyond his control. He finally opened his arms.

"Come here," he said, his voice raspy. "Oh, Memory mine, come here."

She literally flung herself into his embrace, wrapping her arms around his neck as he held her fast, tightly to him. Neither spoke for a long moment as they savored the feel of the one they loved, the one they'd come to believe they would never hold again.

Memory finally tilted her head back to look at him.

"Please forgive me," she whispered.

"It's done, over, put in the past with all that other old news. What's important is now, and all the days and nights to come."

"Will you marry me?" she asked, beginning to smile.

"I think I can fit that into my schedule," he said, the lines of tension easing from his face. "I *am* a busy pecan tree grower, you know. I do love you, Memory, and when I thought I'd lost you, I was one very miserable man. There is nothing that we can't fix if we do it together. Nothing can defeat us."

"I know that now. I'm just grateful that I realized it in time. Drew, I love you, I love you, I love you."

"Ditto," he said, then his mouth melted over hers.

The kiss was deep and rough, speaking of pain, doubts, loneliness, and fears, now dimmed and to be forgotten.

The kiss gentled, declaring love, receiving love, forgiving, rejoicing, reaffirming, and understanding.

And the kiss ignited the still-glowing embers of desire within them, fanning them into a fierce fire of passion.

Drew groaned, "Memory . . ."

"Quickly, Drew," she said, her voice breathless. "Let's go to Memory Mountain and make love in the wildflowers. That was where we first met. That will be where we'll seal our commitment to forever."

"Perfect."

And it was.

On nature's bed of wildflowers they soared up and away from Memory Mountain.

And as they hovered in their private, wondrous place, they were surrounded and serenaded by a multitude of glorious angels singing.

THE EDITOR'S CORNER

Next month LOVESWEPT salutes **MEN IN UNIFORM**, those daring heroes who risk all for life, liberty . . . and the pursuit of women they desire. **MEN IN UNIFORM** are experts at plotting seductive maneuvers, and in six fabulous romances, you'll be at the front lines of passion as each of these men wages a battle for the heart of the woman he loves.

The first of our dashing heroes is Brett Upton in **JUST FRIENDS** by Laura Taylor, LOVESWEPT #600—and he's furious about the attack on Leah Holbrook's life, the attack that cost her her memory and made her forget the love they'd once shared and that he'd betrayed. Now, as he desperately guards her, he dares to believe that fate has given him a second chance to win back the only woman he's ever wanted. Laura will hold you spellbound with this powerful romance.

In **FLYBOY** by Victoria Leigh, LOVESWEPT #601, veteran Air Force pilot Matt Cooper has seen plenty of excitement, but nothing compares to the storm of desire he feels when he rescues Jennifer Delaney from a raging typhoon. Matt has always called the world his home, but the redhead suddenly makes him long to settle down. And with wildfire embraces and whispers of passionate fantasies, he sets out to make the independent beauty share his newfound dream. A splendid love story, told with plenty of Victoria's wit.

Patricia Potter returns to LOVESWEPT with **TROUBA-DOUR**, LOVESWEPT #602. Connor MacLaren is fiercely masculine in a kilt—and from the moment she first lays eyes on him, Leslie Turner feels distinctly overwhelmed. Hired as a publicist for the touring folk-singer, she'd expected anything except this rugged Scot who awakens a reckless hunger she'd never dare confess. But armed with a killer grin and potent kisses, Connor vows to make her surrender to desire. You'll treasure this enchanting romance from Pat.

In her new LOVESWEPT, **HART'S LAW**, #603, Theresa Gladden gives us a sexy sheriff whose smile can melt steel. When Johnny Hart hears that Bailey Asher's coming home, he remembers kissing her breathless the summer she was seventeen—and wonders if she'd still feel so good in his embrace. But Bailey no longer trusts men and she insists on keeping her distance. How Johnny convinces her to open her arms—and heart—to him once more makes for one of Theresa's best LOVESWEPTs.

SURRENDER, BABY, LOVESWEPT #604 by Suzanne Forster, is Geoff Dias's urgent message to Miranda Witherspoon. A soldier of fortune, Geoff has seen and done it all, but nothing burns in his memory more than that one night ten years ago when he'd tasted fierce passion in Miranda's arms. When he agrees to help her find her missing fiancé, he has just one objective in mind: to make her see they're destined only for each other. The way Suzanne writes, the sexual sparks practically leap off the page!

Finally, in **HEALING TOUCH** by Judy Gill, LOVESWEPT #605, army doctor Rob McGee needs a wife to help him raise his young orphaned niece—but what he wants is

Heather Tomasi! He met the lovely temptress only once two years before, but his body still remembers the silk of her skin and the wicked promises in her eyes. She's definitely not marriage material, but Rob has made up his mind. And he'll do anything—even bungee jump—to prove to her that he's the man she needs. Judy will delight you with this wonderful tale.

On sale this month from FANFARE are four fabulous novels. From highly acclaimed author Deborah Smith comes **BLUE WILLOW,** a gloriously heart-stopping love story with characters as passionate and bold as the South that brought them forth. Artemas Colebrook and Lily MacKenzie are bound to each other through the Blue Willow estate . . . and by a passion that could destroy all they have struggled for.

The superstar of the sensual historical, Susan Johnson tempts you with **SINFUL.** Set in the 1780s, Chelsea Ferguson must escape a horrible fate—marriage to a man she doesn't love—by bedding another man. But Sinjin St. John, Duke of Seth, refuses to be her rescuer and Chelsea must resort to a desperate deception that turns into a passionate adventure.

Bestselling LOVESWEPT author Helen Mittermeyer has penned **THE PRINCESS OF THE VEIL,** a breathtakingly romantic tale set in long-ago Scotland and Iceland. When Viking princess Iona is captured by the notorious Scottish chief Magnus Sinclair, she vows never to belong to him, though he would make her his bride.

Theresa Weir, author of the widely praised **FOREVER,** delivers a new novel of passion and drama. In **LAST SUMMER,** movie star Johnnie Irish returns to his Texas hometown, intent on getting revenge. But all thoughts of getting even disappear when he meets the beautiful widow Maggie Mayfield.

Also on sale this month in the hardcover edition from Doubleday is **SACRED LIES** by Dianne Edouard and Sandra Ware. In this sexy contemporary novel, Romany Chase must penetrate the inner sanctum of the Vatican on a dangerous mission . . . and walk a fine line between two men who could be friend or foe.

Happy reading!

With warmest wishes,

Nita Taublib

Nita Taublib
Associate Publisher
LOVESWEPT and FANFARE

Don't miss these fabulous
Bantam
Women's Fiction
titles
on sale in JANUARY

BLUE WILLOW
by Deborah Smith

SINFUL
by Susan Johnson

PRINCESS OF THE VEIL
by Helen Mittermeyer

LAST SUMMER
by Theresa Weir

In hardcover from Doubleday,
SACRED LIES
by Dianne Edouard and Sandra Ware
authors of MORTAL SINS

BLUE WILLOW
by
Deborah Smith
author of MIRACLE

"Extraordinary talent . . . [BLUE WILLOW is] a complex and emotionally wrenching tale that sweeps readers on an intense rollercoaster ride through the gamut of human emotions."   —*Romantic Times*

There had always been MacKenzies and Colebrooks at Blue Willow, their histories entangled like the graceful branches of the rare willow trees that thrived there. Artemas Colebrook had always loved the decaying estate in the lush hills of Georgia, but his soul was bound forever to the land the day the boy held tiny Lily MacKenzie minutes after her birth. Though he was torn from Blue Willow by the crumbling Colebrook fortune, Artemas swore that he would return someday—to Blue Willow . . . and to Lily.

A heartwrenching tragedy has brought Lily back to the tiny farm where she spent her childhood—a tragedy that has made Artemas's brothers and sisters her bitter enemies. Torn between family loyalties and their shared sense of destiny, Artemas and Lily must come to terms with a childhood devotion that has turned to bittersweet desire, a passion that could destroy all they have struggled for—even Blue Willow itself.

The following excerpt is an unusual one, but it gives a perfect introduction to young Artemas who grows up to become an absolutely wonderful hero in BLUE WILLOW. . . .

MacKenzie, Georgia, 1962

Artemas was only seven years old, but he knew a lot of secrets, most of them bewildering and terrible.

Uncle Charles had big balls and a tight ass. That was one secret. Father said so. Artemas must never again ask President Kennedy to arm-wrestle when the president was visiting at Uncle Charles's house, because it embarrassed Uncle Charles. Uncle Charles was the only Colebrook who'd inherited the Family Business Sense, and that was why Grandmother let him run the Colebrook China Company. She owned it but nobody asked her to do any work. That was another secret.

Father had married Mother for her money. Mother was half-Spanish, and Spaniards were Failed Royalty, whatever that was, but Mother was also, as Father put it, a Gold-Plated Philadelphia Hughs. What upset Father was that she'd done some mysterious bad things with money, and that had made Grandfather and Grandmother Hughs mad, so they'd stopped owning her, they'd Dis-Owned her, and her money had gone to Aunt Lucille, who'd married a Texas oilman and moved to a ranch, where people said she was raising children and hell.

Artemas loved Mother and Father desperately. That was no secret, but his love couldn't erase their frightening moods or the whispered words he'd heard once among the servants at Port's Heart, the home Grandfather Hughs had given them, by the ocean on Long Island.

The children will be marked for life.

Other secrets were trickier. No one told him they were secrets; he decided on his own. He'd rather die than reveal what he'd seen his parents do once in the gazebo at Port's Heart, after the bank men from New York drove away with boxes full of Father's important papers. Artemas, playing in the roses nearby, had been too frightened and horrified to let his parents know he was there.

Father and Mother had yelled at each other about money. Then Father tore Mother's skirt open and shoved her down on the gazebo's hard marble floor. Mother slapped Father, and Father hit her back until she screamed. Then he opened the front of his pants, got on top of her, and pushed down between her legs so hard that she began crying. He bumped up and down on her. Then he said, "You're as worthless as I am, you spoiled bitch."

The next day Mother cut up all her ball gowns with a pair of garden clippers. Then she bought new ones. There always seemed to be money for what Mother and Father wanted, particularly for clothes, parties, and travel. Father was on the board of Colebrook China, but Uncle Charles didn't ask him to do much, and he had plenty of free time.

The currents swirling around his family frightened Artemas. Only one place was safe from them.

Blue Willow. For the past two years Artemas had spent his holidays and summers there, with grand, dignified Grandmother Colebrook.

Blue Willow was a lost kingdom, with ruined outbuildings, dark forests, and overgrown fields to explore, and in the center was an enormous, echo-filled mansion perfect for a seven-year-old's fantasies, all hidden safely in the wild, watchful mountains of Georgia. Zea MacKenzie, the housekeeper, her husband, Drew, the gardener, and Drew's parents lived on their farm in the hollow beyond the mansion's lake and hills, along the ancient Cherokee trail. They were poor, Grandmother said, but they were MacKenzies, and that would always make them special.

Grandmother was special too. People whispered that when she was young she'd been something called a Ziegfeld Girl, before she became a Golddigger and married Grandfather. Grandfather had slipped and fallen out a window on Wall Street during the Depression, so to help Grandmother after he died, his sisters took Father and Uncle Charles away from her.

They told Grandmother she could stay at Blue Willow, and they'd raise her sons for her, in New York. She'd been at Blue Willow ever since. Which was fine with Artemas, because it meant he could visit her. Grandmother said he was her Consolation Prize, and he liked the sound of that.

But she was too old to keep up with a little boy all the time, so she turned him over to the wonderful MacKenzies. He loved them and felt loved by them in a way that made him feel frantic with guilt and confusion when he thought of his parents. Every day with the MacKenzies was an adventure. If being poor only meant that you had to live on a farm like theirs, he wanted to be their kind of poor.

The Colebrooks were poor now, too, but in a different way. They looked rich enough, but people felt sorry for them behind their backs. That was one of the secrets he must keep, Grandmother said.

Without money, all a Colebrook had was the Right Friends and an Important Name. Mother said that was enough, if you knew who to suck up to.

Artemas decided to avoid learning more family secrets if he could help it.

SINFUL
by
Susan Johnson
author of BLAZE and FORBIDDEN

"One of romance's hottest stars, Susan Johnson is in rare form in SINFUL, a highly sensual love story. . . . Titillating, scintillating, tension-filled and brimming over with heated love scenes . . . SINFUL is just that—sinfully enjoyable. Indulge yourself and your fantasies." —*Romantic Times*

Sweeping from 1780s Europe to the forbidden salons of a Tunisian harem, SINFUL tells the tale of a heroine determined to soil her reputation . . . and the noble rake who refuses to assist her.

Chelsea took a deep breath, looked out over the panorama of Cambridgeshire before her, returned her gaze to Sinjin's face, and quickly, before she lost her nerve, blurted out, "Would it be possible to consider this a business arrangement?"

"How much?" he presciently said with a faint smile, familiar with "business arrangements," beguiled by her sudden agitation. How charming she looked, blushing and flustered, riding bareback in a worn skirt and boy's jacket, her booted legs exposed with her skirt hitched up, one pink knee close enough to touch.

She inhaled and held her breath for a moment while he admired the fullness of her breasts constrained by the green velvet boy's coat. Then, exhaling in a great sigh, she admitted, "I can't say it."

"Fifty thousand?" he graciously suggested.

She glanced up sharply. "How did you know?"

"Your wager, darling. Obviously you're in need of fifty thousand."

"I'm not," she quickly interjected, "but my father is, you see," and then it all tumbled out—the eighty thousand he owed the money-lenders, the hopes to sell Thune if he won tomorrow, the deduction for that sale, then the remainder she was hoping she could raise from her . . .

"Business arrangement," Sinjin gently offered when she hesitated over the wording.

"I'd be ever so grateful," she added touchingly, and for the briefest moment, Sinjin considered giving her the money, as a gentleman would, without requiring her company for a week.

The brief moment passed, however, and more selfish motives intervened, having to do with the bewitching young lady short inches away, with rosy cheeks, golden wind-blown hair, an unearthly beauty, and a warm spirited nature that somehow seduced more boldly than the most celebrated belles of the Ton.

He would have her. On ungentlemanly terms. At any price.

"Would you like a down payment . . . now?"

"Oh no, I trust you."

Her words were so naive that he experienced a transient pang of conscience—quickly overcome. "In that case, consider the fifty thousand yours at next week's end."

"Thank you very much, Your Grace," she softly said. Her smile was angelic and dazzling at the same time, typical of the curious power she possessed to project both innocence and the most disarmingly opulent sexuality.

And at that moment, only heroic gentlemanly restraint—which proved, he thought, that he at least had a conscience, albeit infrequently used—kept him in the saddle. Of course, it would have been extremely embarrassing for him to stand at the moment, doeskin breeches more a second skin than enveloping raiment. "The pleasure's mine," he softly said with a certain degree of sincere feeling and smiled back at her.

Should she tell him she was flattered? Chelsea wondered, forcing back the chuckle that threatened to explode, aware of the Duke's arousal, equally aware of his unutterably beautiful smile that lit up his eyes, crinkled across his graceful cheekbones, tilted the corners of his mouth. Seductively.

"You're one flashy lad," she said with a grin, her gaze drifting downward suggestively. "Do you think you can wait a week?"

"Hell, no," he lazily drawled, his own grin in place. "Do I have to?"

She leaned back, propping herself on one elbow, looking very small on Thune's broad frame. "I'm verra tempted," she teased, dropping into a soft Scottish burr, her dark-lashed violet eyes traveling slowly down Sinjin's powerful body.

"Will Thune stay?"

At her nod, he threw a leg over Mameluke's neck, slid to the ground and, reaching up, lifted her off Thune. He didn't ask permission and she felt no constraint. His concern was obvious; in fact, he scanned the horizon with a minute scrutiny before taking her hand and leading her toward a small flat table rock. Initials had been carved in the soft sandstone by generations past, and he contemplated them with a brief distracted look before lifting her up and seating her.

"Tell me."

He shook his head. "Not for lady's ears."

"Do I look like a lady?" Chelsea retorted, piqued at being treated like a child.

Sinjin gazed at her for a long moment in her old tan serge skirt and short boy's jacket, his blue eyes as azure-luminous as the sky. "Oh yes," he said, low and husky. "Definitely. Absolutely. From a mile away."

His voice touched her like the summer sun, warmed her skin, heated her blood. His fingers stopped stroking her hands and curled protectively around them. "Are all Scottish lasses like you?" he whispered, his question tentative, inquiring beyond the simple query, for he wanted her like a schoolboy, without discipline or reason.

"Are all Sassenachs like you?" she whispered back, lifting her face for a kiss, feeling as he did . . . overpowered and out of control.

His mouth was smiling when he kissed her, and he murmured against the softness of her lips, "All the mamas hope not . . ."

But all the young ladies would be willing, Chelsea didn't doubt— mamas or not. And she swayed into the kiss, wanting to take what he offered.

He moved swiftly to steady her from falling, his hands gentle on her shoulders, and lifting his mouth, he murmured, "You ride the same way . . . recklessly."

"And fast," she softly replied, reaching for the buttons on his breeches.

"And wild . . ." He had the top three buttons on her jacket loose.

"And wild." She wanted him inside her, now, this instant; she wanted to feel the bliss, the hot, drenching rush of sensation.

He lifted her down then, for despite his carnal urgency, he

preferred a less exhibitionist position than atop a table rock on the crest of a hill visible for miles. Perhaps too he was protecting himself, an ingrained instinct for the most eligible bachelor in the kingdom.

The grass was soft, the huge sandstone monolith a shield from prying eyes, but Sinjin swiftly surveyed the surrounding landscape like a wolf scenting the wind before he returned his attention to Chelsea.

"There's no one about," she whispered, her jacket undone, her skirt flared out around her, a lush, nubile young maid fresh as spring green grass wanting him.

He recognized that look in a woman's eyes, that heated stage that ignored husbands or too observant servants, the kind that considered garden houses at breakfast routs sufficiently private. The kind that required he keep one foot against the door—which he was eminently proficient at. So he smiled his agreement instead of pointing out that someone could ride up from the far horizon in very short order. And reaching out, he brushed her opened jacket away from her breasts. "You're not cold." A hint of a smile played across his mouth.

"Au contraire," Chelsea whispered. She was so warm that the cool breeze was comfort to her bared flesh. Desire burned through her body. He had only to approach her and she wanted him; he had only to smile that slow lazy smile and she melted.

"Are you in a hurry?" He was asking how much time he had, but the lingering trail of his fingers circling her pink nipples distracted her, excited her, conferred a certain ambiguity to his query.

"Yes," she whispered, "and . . . no . . ." A small, languorous smile curved her lips, touched her eyes, lent a bewitching sensuality to the delicate beauty of her face. "And I hope you can accommodate both answers."

"With pleasure," he softly replied, "and beginning with the— yes . . ." he added, his dark lashes half-covering his eyes as he unbuttoned the remainder of the closings on his doeskin. "I'm at your service . . ."

PRINCESS OF THE VEIL
by
Helen Mittermeyer

We are proud to publish the first historical romance from one of your favorite LOVESWEPT authors!

"Intrigue, a fascinating setting, high adventure, a wonderful love story and steamy sensuality turn PRINCESS OF THE VEIL into a truly delicious summer treat. This is fine entertainment from a new voice on the [historical romance] scene." —*Romantic Times*

A proud Viking princess is pitted against a lusty Scottish chieftain in a duel of wits, courage, and passion. In the following scene, the Viking crew of her ship has just been overwhelmed by Scots when Princess Iona takes matters into her own hands. . . .

"'Tis my people's safety I would have," Iona called. "Swear by God that you'll grant this or I'll drive this sword through his skull."

After an endless moment, a bronze-haired man moved. Sword in hand, he strode into the water, then leaped up onto the Viking boat. Iona stood motionless, watching as he walked toward her along the oars.

"I am Sinclair," he said, and stepped onto the next oar. "It would seem you wish to be a warrior. Fight me then, Viking. If you win, your people go free. If I win . . ." He shrugged, and his hair glinted fire in the sun.

"Agreed," she said. "I'll pick up your gauntlet, Scot. 'Tis my right to choose the time and the weapons." She paused and stared at the giant, who was as comely as the devil. Then she smiled as the thrill of the challenge raced through her. "I choose now!" she suddenly shouted. "And oar running!"

Before the Scot could move, Iona jumped up into the air and landed hard on the oar where she'd been standing. Instantly, her feet began a running cadence that would keep the heavy oar straight and spinning. The object of oar running was to spin the oars until one person overbalanced and fell.

The Scot hesitated only a moment before he too jumped on his oar and began running. Iona watched him critically as she recalled every lesson she'd ever learned.

Long ago the perils and tricks of the sport had been drilled into her. A slap from the oars could break a limb or crack her skull; a misstep could send her crashing down on a spinning oar, maiming or killing her. She forced away those thoughts and concentrated on her other lessons—the speed needed to keep the oar parallel with the water, what would make it rise or fall, the best balance for using a weapon, when to strike, to feint, to back off. More times than she could count she'd been dumped in the frigid waters of BorgarFjord. But she'd struggled on until she'd mastered the skill, until she'd been able to stay on longer than some of the best Vikings, managing even to dunk them a time or two.

It took Iona only minutes to realize that her opponent had run the oars more than once. He was good, but not as good as she. He had strength, determination, and agility on his side, while she had the edge of her well-honed skill.

He often tried to reach her with the flat of his sword. She stayed just far enough away and speeded up, so that he'd have to do the same in order to prevent a collision of oars. If hers spun faster it would be atop his, giving her the advantage.

Magnus watched the Viking woman closely. She was damned good, and he hadn't expected that. Hell, he hadn't expected her to take up his challenge. She was a woman, outnumbered, her people's weapons down. But what a warrior she was. She looked as fragile as the silk that had been swathed around her head and now flew like a banner behind her. She was a beauty too. Silver and gold sparked her hair and skin, and her eyes were like the green leaves of summer, or like—

Damn! Her beauty had distracted him, and she'd almost toppled him. She was able to control her oar well. Ah! He could reach her. He tapped her backside with the flat of his sword, thinking to take her down, but she danced out of his way, her movements as sprightly as a nymph's. He'd get her, though. And maybe he'd keep her.

Iona saw the sudden dangerous glitter in his eyes and swore. The Scot might not intend to kill her, but he did intend to win. She had to do something soon, or he'd have her. There was one maneuver, perhaps unknown to him, that her father had called mortally perilous. Calling on the Holy Virgin, Christ, and Wotan, she made her decision.

She stared down at the whirling oar, counting every other beat. It had to be just right, or she'd break her leg.

"Wotan!" she shouted, and the age-old war cry was answered by her Vikings. Then she leapt high and came down hard on her opponent's oar. The landing jarred every tooth in her head, rattling through her like a blow. The instant her feet hit, she began running backward, the motion sending every muscle in her body screeching in pain and protest and wrenching a curse from her.

Could she hold on? Only if she'd caught him off guard enough, so that he couldn't bring his superior strength into play. Surprise flashed across his face, and she bore down with all her strength, spinning the oar as hard as she could.

The oar quivered, warning that the Scot was off balance. Pain spasmed in her back and neck as the Vikings roared behind her. They saw her advantage and sensed what she intended to do with it.

Iona increased her speed as she moved closer to him. Hefting the heavy sword, she swung it slowly, catching him on the arm. At the same moment, she jumped up and down, reversing once more, the action slamming through her head and body. The quick change sent the heavy oar splashing downward. She dug in, curling her toes around the wood. The Scot comprehended the ploy and fought for purchase, but he lost it.

Incredulity, fury, and stupefaction chased across his face as his sword flew from his hand. Then he spun in the air and fell backward into the sea.

The Scots cried out in anguish, and several men leapt up to grab his sword before it could follow him.

The Sinclair surfaced, and Iona easily saw both the anger and the vengeance in his eyes. "You win, Viking," he shouted up to her. "Your *people* shall be free. But *you* are my prisoner."

LAST SUMMER
by
Theresa Weir
author of FOREVER
and winner of two *Romantic Times* Awards

*Set amid the glittering lights of Hollywood and the desert heat of Hope,
Texas, LAST SUMMER is the emotionally powerful tale of a bad-boy
actor and the beautiful widow who tames his heart. Driven out of his
hometown, Hope, Johnnie Irish finds instant success in the movies and
makes headlines with his outlandish behavior. When circumstances force
him to return to Hope, he has revenge in mind. But all thoughts of getting
even disappear when he meets local resident Maggie Mayfield.*

*In the following excerpt, Johnnie, who has volunteered to play the piano
for a show Maggie is directing, threatens to leave in the middle of
rehearsals.*

"Are you saying if we had sex you'd stay?"

His anger softened a little, was replaced by an equally unflatter-
ing smugness. "That depends."

"On what?"

"On whether or not you're a good lay."

She'd never slapped anybody in her life. Until now, it had always
seemed an immature and overly emotional thing to do. She raised
a hand and swung. Hard.

His reflexes were quick. He blocked, his fingers locking around
her wrist. The impact of the deflected blow sent a jarring vibration
all the way up her arm to her shoulder socket.

"That's something you'll never know," she said through gritted
teeth. "Whether I'm good or not. I want to go down in history as
being the only woman in America you haven't screwed."

He laughed, but there was no humor in the sound. He was still
holding her wrist high in the air. He pulled her close, his body

slamming against hers, almost knocking the wind out of her. His other hand pressed against her lower spine. If anyone were to come in, it would look as though they were performing some bizarre dance.

"You're a self-righteous hypocrite," he said, his voice soft, threatening. In his eyes she read unshakable determination.

She tried to jerk away, but he held her fast. Suddenly his leg was behind hers, pushing at the back of her knees, making her fold. Her wrist slipped free of his grip. Arms behind her, she caught herself as her bottom hit the polished floor.

He dropped to his knees beside her, moving to cover her with his body. Before he could make contact, she scrambled backward across the floor.

His hand lashed out, grabbing her ankle, dragging her back to him.

"Let go of me! I hate you!" she screamed.

He pulled her underneath him. He held her down with his weight, forcing her legs apart, insinuating himself between her thighs.

She raised a hand to hit him once more. He grabbed it, stopping her. Off balance, they rolled until she was on top, her legs splayed on either side of his hips, her heaving breasts crushed to his rapidly rising and falling chest.

And as Johnnie stared up at her, he could see that her anger and hate were gone. Now there was only fear.

His own anger dissolved. He let go of her arms, closed his eyes, and let his head drop to the floor.

"Go ahead, hit me," he said, suddenly weary of the whole thing. "W-what?"

"Hit me. I won't stop you this time."

Now that his eyes were closed, all of his senses were focused on his painful erection, throbbing against his zipper, against her warmth. Even without his eyes closed, he could remember how she felt. All soft. And warm. And wet.

Her weight shifted. She shoved herself upright, causing her pelvis to press against him even more, giving him even more of a pleasurable pain.

He groaned, just managing to keep his hands from cupping her bottom and grinding her into him. He had to have release. He'd never been in this kind of situation, where he couldn't get release.

Then her weight was completely gone, but he was still in agony. He flung an arm over his face, waiting for his body to calm down, his breathing to quiet, his muscles to relax.

Finally he opened his eyes.

She was standing a few feet away, her arms crossed at her chest, one leg straight, one hip out, her face flushed, hair hanging down her neck, having come loose from the band at the back of her head.

"Why are you leaving?" she asked.

He had to give her credit for trying to put things back on track. But damned if he'd tell her about Cahill and what had happened last night. It was too degrading. He just wanted to forget about it. He just wanted to get the hell out of Hope as fast as he could. "I told you, I'm bored."

"*When* are you leaving?"

"Right away. I'm driving to El Paso, then catching a flight to California." He needed to get going. He'd stayed too long already. Now that their wrestling match was over, the claustrophobic feeling he'd been fighting all day was coming back.

"What would make you stay?"

He didn't answer.

"Sex. Would you stay for sex?"

He drew in a breath, almost choking. "What?"

"You heard me. What if I told you I'd have sex with you if you stayed?"

He let out his breath. "Then I'd say you were bluffing."

She frowned.

But she was right about one thing. He wanted her. He'd like to have her at least once before he left.

He shoved himself to his feet and faced her. He didn't understand it, but he suddenly had the urge to touch her, not in a sexual way, but a comforting way. Just for the sake of touching her.

"If we ever do make love," he said, silently moving toward her, "it will be because you want to, and I want to."

He did touch her then, a palm to the side of her blood-warm face. Surprisingly she didn't move away. She simply stared at him, lips parted. He couldn't resist. He kissed her. Not a soft, gentle kiss, but a possessive kiss, his tongue quickly outlining her lips before plunging inside to stroke the wetness of her mouth. Her breasts were pressed to his chest. He could feel the hardness of each nipple, feel himself rising again, straining against the seam of his jeans.

One hand came down to cup her bottom. He lifted her into him, making sure she could feel him. Then he pulled his mouth from hers. "I'll stay," he told her, staring into her wide amber eyes. "But not because of some bargain."

He couldn't help but feel a twinge of self-mockery. His present attitude toward sex was a little different from the one he'd had only a month ago. And he supposed he should give Maggie credit for that.

She was still watching him, still pressed to him, one hand gripping his shirtsleeve, her eyes full of confusion and a sort of bemused wonder.

He kissed her again. Quickly this time, before he was tempted to pull her to the floor and make love to her so she wouldn't forget him.

He could put up with Hope, Texas, for three more days. And three more nights. He would survive the nightmares. The tossing and turning and trying to forget. He would do it for Maggie.

OFFICIAL RULES TO WINNERS CLASSIC SWEEPSTAKES

No Purchase necessary. To enter the sweepstakes follow instructions found elsewhere in this offer. You can also enter the sweepstakes by hand printing your name, address, city, state and zip code on a 3" x 5" piece of paper and mailing it to: Winners Classic Sweepstakes, P.O. Box 785, Gibbstown, NJ 08027. Mail each entry separately. Sweepstakes begins 12/1/91. Entries must be received by 6/1/93. Some presentations of this sweepstakes may feature a deadline for the Early Bird prize. If the offer you receive does, then to be eligible for the Early Bird prize your entry must be received according to the Early Bird date specified. Not responsible for lost, late, damaged, misdirected, illegible or postage due mail. Mechanically reproduced entries are not eligible. All entries become property of the sponsor and will not be returned.

Prize Selection/Validations: Winners will be selected in random drawings on or about 7/30/93, by VENTURA ASSOCIATES, INC., an independent judging organization whose decisions are final. Odds of winning are determined by total number of entries received. Circulation of this sweepstakes is estimated not to exceed 200 million. Entrants need not be present to win. All prizes are guaranteed to be awarded and delivered to winners. Winners will be notified by mail and may be required to complete an affidavit of eligibility and release of liability which must be returned within 14 days of date of notification or alternate winners will be selected. Any guest of a trip winner will also be required to execute a release of liability. Any prize notification letter or any prize returned to a participating sponsor, Bantam Doubleday Dell Publishing Group, Inc., its participating divisions or subsidiaries, or VENTURA ASSOCIATES, INC. as undeliverable will be awarded to an alternate winner. Prizes are not transferable. No multiple prize winners except as may be necessary due to unavailability, in which case a prize of equal or greater value will be awarded. Prizes will be awarded approximately 90 days after the drawing. All taxes, automobile license and registration fees, if applicable, are the sole responsibility of the winners. Entry constitutes permission (except where prohibited) to use winners' names and likenesses for publicity purposes without further or other compensation.

Participation: This sweepstakes is open to residents of the United States and Canada, except for the province of Quebec. This sweepstakes is sponsored by Bantam Doubleday Dell Publishing Group, Inc. (BDD), 666 Fifth Avenue, New York, NY 10103. Versions of this sweepstakes with different graphics will be offered in conjunction with various solicitations or promotions by different subsidiaries and divisions of BDD. Employees and their families of BDD, its division, subsidiaries, advertising agencies, and VENTURA ASSOCIATES, INC., are not eligible.

Canadian residents, in order to win, must first correctly answer a time limited arithmetical skill testing question. Void in Quebec and wherever prohibited or restricted by law. Subject to all federal, state, local and provincial laws and regulations.

Prizes: The following values for prizes are determined by the manufacturers' suggested retail prices or by what these items are currently known to be selling for at the time this offer was published. Approximate retail values include handling and delivery of prizes. Estimated maximum retail value of prizes: 1 Grand Prize ($27,500 if merchandise or $25,000 Cash); 1 First Prize ($3,000); 5 Second Prizes ($400 each); 35 Third Prizes ($100 each); 1,000 Fourth Prizes ($9.00 each) ; 1 Early Bird Prize ($5,000); Total approximate maximum retail value is $50,000. Winners will have the option of selecting any prize offered at level won. Automobile winner must have a valid driver's license at the time the car is awarded. Trips are subject to space and departure availability. Certain black-out dates may apply. Travel must be completed within one year from the time the prize is awarded. Minors must be accompanied by an adult. Prizes won by minors will be awarded in the name of parent or legal guardian.

For a list of Major Prize Winners (available after 7/30/93): send a self-addressed, stamped envelope entirely separate from your entry to: Winners Classic Sweepstakes Winners, P.O. Box 825, Gibbstown, NJ 08027. Requests must be received by 6/1/93. DO NOT SEND ANY OTHER CORRESPONDENCE TO THIS P.O. BOX.

FANFARE

Bestselling Women's Fiction

Sandra Brown

_____ 29783-X A WHOLE NEW LIGHT ..... $5.99/6.99 in Canada
_____ 29500-4 TEXAS! SAGE $4.99/5.99
_____ 29085-1 22 INDIGO PLACE $4.50/5.50
_____ 28990-X TEXAS! CHASE $4.99/5.99
_____ 28951-9 TEXAS! LUCKY $4.99/5.99

Amanda Quick

_____ 29325-7 RENDEZVOUS $4.99/5.99
_____ 28354-5 SEDUCTION $4.99/5.99
_____ 28932-2 SCANDAL $4.95/5.95
_____ 28594-7 SURRENDER..................................... $4.50/5.50

Nora Roberts

_____ 29597-7 CARNAL INNOCENCE $5.50/6.50
_____ 29078-9 GENUINE LIES.................................. $4.99/5.99
_____ 28578-5 PUBLIC SECRETS $4.95/5.95
_____ 26461-3 HOT ICE $4.99/5.99
_____ 26574-1 SACRED SINS $5.50/6.50
_____ 27859-2 SWEET REVENGE $5.50/6.50
_____ 27283-7 BRAZEN VIRTUE................................ $4.99/5.99

Iris Johansen

_____ 29871-2 LAST BRIDGE HOME $4.50/5.50
_____ 29604-3 THE GOLDEN BARBARIAN $4.99/5.99
_____ 29244-7 REAP THE WIND $4.99/5.99
_____ 29032-0 STORM WINDS $4.99/5.99
_____ 28855-5 THE WIND DANCER............................ $4.95/5.95

Ask for these titles at your bookstore or use this page to order.